AF521085

Sons Of Fire

A Novel

Vol. II

by

M. E. Braddon

Double 9 BOOKS

Sons Of Fire

A Novel

Vol. II

by M. E. Braddon

ISBN: 978-93-70819-90-0

Published by

DOUBLE 9 BOOKS
2/13-B, Ansari Road
Daryaganj, New Delhi – 110002
info@double9books.com
www.double9books.com
Tel. 011-40042856

ABOUT THE AUTHOR

Mary Elizabeth Braddon (1835–1915) was an English novelist, best known for her sensationalist novels during the Victorian era. Her 1862 novel Lady Audley's Secret is particularly famous, earning her widespread recognition and cementing her place in literary history. Braddon's works often dealt with themes of hidden secrets, psychological tension, and societal norms, becoming widely popular with Victorian readers.

She was born in London and had a varied career, initially acting before turning to writing. Her work often blended romance, mystery, and drama, and she became a key figure in the genre of sensation novels. Braddon's personal life was also colorful; she had a long relationship with her publisher, John Maxwell, whom she married in 1874. She had two children, both of whom also pursued literary careers.

Braddon's influence on Victorian fiction was significant, and her works were admired for their compelling plots and ability to explore darker aspects of human nature, often challenging the moral and social codes of her time. She passed away at the age of 79 in Richmond, leaving behind a legacy that continues to be appreciated in both literary and popular contexts.

CONTENTS

CHAPTER I
FATE INTERVENES 7

CHAPTER II
"BEFORE THE NIGHT BE FALLEN ACROSS THY WAY" 15

CHAPTER III
WHILE LEAVES WERE FALLING 22

CHAPTER IV
"LET NO MAN LIVE AS I HAVE LIVED" 31

CHAPTER V
"CHANCE CANNOT CHANGE MY LOVE, NOR TIME IMPAIR" 38

CHAPTER VI
AT EVENSONG 46

CHAPTER VII
"THE DEAD MAN TOUCH'D ME FROM THE PAST" 50

CHAPTER VIII
"WHAT WAS A SPECK EXPANDS INTO A STAR" 66

CHAPTER IX
"A WHITE STAR MADE OF MEMORY LONG AGO" 83

CHAPTER X
"AND THAT UNREST WHICH MEN MISCALL DELIGHT" 99

CHAPTER XI
"WHO KNOWS WHY LOVE BEGINS?" 108

CHAPTER XII
"THAT WAY MADNESS LIES" 115

CHAPTER I
FATE INTERVENES

The return of Geoffrey Wornock made no essential difference in the lives of the lovers. Suzette continued her organ practice; Allan continued his visits to the Manor House; and Suzette and Allan were much oftener Mrs. Wornock's companions than her son, whose restless temper did not allow of his remaining long in any one place, and for whom monotony of any kind was intolerable.

He stayed in London for a week buying horses, and having brought home a string of four, every one supposed to be matchless, he began hunting with the vigour of a man whose appetite for that British sport had only been sharpened by paper-chases and polo in the tropics. Not content with the South Sarum, he travelled up and down the line, hunted with the Vine from Basingstoke, and with the H. H. from Winchester. He was up and away in the grey November mornings after a seven-o'clock breakfast, and seldom home in time for an eight-o'clock dinner.

On the days when there was no hunting to be had, he flung himself into the delights of the music-room with all the ardour of a musical fanatic, and Allan and Suzette were content to listen in meek astonishment to performances which were far above the drawing-room amateur, although marked by certain imperfections and carelessnesses which seemed inevitable in a player whose ardour was too fitful for the drudgery of daily practice.

These musical days were the bright spots in Mrs. Wornock's existence, the chief bond of union between mother and son; as if music were the only spell which could hold this volatile spirit within the circle of domestic love.

"I like my mother to accompany me," said Geoffrey. "I have played with some prodigious swells, but not one of them has had her sympathetic touch, her instantaneous comprehension of my spontaneities. They expected me to be faultily faultless, instead of which I play de Beriot as Chopin used to play Chopin, indulging every caprice as to time."

Geoffrey was occasionally present when one of the organ lessons was in progress. He was interested, but not so much so as to sit still and listen.

He carried Allan off to the billiard-room, or the stable, before the lesson was half over.

"What a happy little family we are," he said laughingly one day, as he and Allan were strolling stablewards. "My mother is almost as fond of your *fiancée* as if she were her daughter."

"Your mother is a very amiable woman, as well as a gifted woman."

"Gifted? yes, that's the word. She is all enthusiasm. There have been no spiritualists or supernatural people here lately, I suppose?"

"No."

"I'm glad of that. My poor mother loses her head when that kind of people are in the way. She is ready to believe in their nonsense. She wants to believe. She wants to see visions and dream dreams. She has secluded herself from the world of the living, and she would give half her fortune if she could bring the dead into her drawing-room. Poor dear mother! How many weary hours she has spent waiting for materializations that have never materialized! I have never been able to convince her that all her spiritualistic friends are pretenders and comedians. She tells me she knows that some are charlatans; but she believes that their theories are based upon eternal truths. She rebukes my scepticism with an appeal to the Witch of Endor. I dare not shock her by confessing that I have my doubts even about the Witch of Endor."

He had a way of making light of his mother's fancies and eccentricities which had in its gaiety no touch of disrespect. Gaiety was the chief characteristic of his temperament, as it was with Suzette. He brought a new element of mirthfulness into the life at Discombe Manor; but with this happy temperament there was the drawback of an eager desire for change and movement which disturbed the atmosphere of a house whose chief charm to Allan's mind had been its sober quiet, its atmosphere of old-world peace.

Allan studied this young man's character closely, studied him and thought of him much more than he wanted to think of him, and vainly struggled against an uneasy feeling that in every superiority of this new acquaintance there lurked a danger to his own happiness.

"He is handsomer than I am," mused Allan, in one of his despondent moods. "He has a gayer temper—Suzette's own temper—which sees all things in the happiest light. I sit and watch them, listen to them, and feel myself worlds away from them both; and yet if she were free to-morrow he could never love her as I love her. There, at least, I am the superior. He has no such power of concentration as I have. To his frivolous nature no woman could ever be all in all."

These despondent moods were luckily not of long duration. On Suzette's part there had not been the faintest sign of wavering; and Allan felt ashamed of the jealous fears which fell ever and anon like a black cloud across the sunny prospect of his life. However valiantly he might struggle against that lurking jealousy, there were occasions upon which he could not master it, and his darkest hours were those during which he sat in the music-room at Discombe, and heard Suzette and Geoffrey playing concertante duets for violin and piano. It seemed to him as the violinist bent over the pretty dark head, to turn a leaf, or to explain a passage in the piano score, that for these two there was a language which he knew not, a language in which mind spoke to mind, and perhaps heart to heart. Who could keep the heart altogether out of the question when that most eloquent of all languages was making its impassioned appeal? Every long-drawn legato chord upon the Strad, every delicate diminuendo of the sighing strings, the tremulous bow so lightly held in the long lissom fingers, sounded like an avowal.

"I love you, I love you, I love you," sobbed the violin; "how can you care for that dumb brute yonder, while I am telling my love in heavenliest sounds, in strains that thrill along every nerve, and tremble at the door of your heart? How can you care for that dumb dog, or care how you hurt him by your inconstancy?"

Possessed by these evil fancies, Allan started up from his seat in a remote window, and began to pace the room in the midst of a de Beriot sonata, to which Suzette had been promoted after a good deal of practice in less brilliant music.

"What's the matter, old fellow?" asked Geoffrey, noting that impatient promenade; "was I out of tune?"

"No, you were only too much in tune."

"How do you mean? I don't understand——"

"Is it likely you can understand me—or I you?" cried Allan, impetuously. "You have a language which I have not, a sense which is lacking in me. You and Suzette are in a paradise whose gate I can't open. Don't think me an envious, churlish kind of fellow, if I sometimes grudge you your happiness."

"But, my dear Allan, you are fond of music—you like listening——"

"No, I don't. I have had too much listening, too much of being out of it. Put on your hat, Suzette, and come for a walk. I am tired to death of your de Beriot."

Mrs. Wornock was sitting a little way from the piano, reading. She looked up wonderingly at this outburst. Never before had Allan been guilty of such rough speech in her presence. Never before had he spoken with such rude authority to Suzette.

"If our music has not the good fortune to please you, I would suggest that there are several rooms in this house where you would not hear it," said Geoffrey, laying down his fiddle.

All the brightness had faded from his countenance, leaving it very pale. Suzette looked from one to the other with an expression of piteous distress. The two young men stood looking at each other, Allan flushed and fiery, Geoffrey's pallid face fixed and stern, with an anger which was stronger than the occasion warranted. They were sufficiently alike to make any ill-will between them seem like a brother's quarrel.

"You are very good, but I would rather be out-of-doors. Are you coming, Suzette?"

"Not till I have finished the sonata," she answered quietly, with a look which reproved his rudeness, and then began to play.

Geoffrey took up his fiddle, and the performance was resumed as if nothing had happened.

Mrs. Wornock rose and went to Allan.

"Will you come for a stroll with me, Allan?" she asked, taking up the warm Indian shawl which lay on a chair near the window. "It is not too cold for the garden."

He could not refuse such an invitation as this, though it tortured him to leave those two alone at the piano. He opened the window, wrapped Mrs. Wornock in her shawl, and followed her to the lawn.

"Allan, why were you angry just now?" she asked.

"Why? Perhaps I had better tell you the truth. I am miserable when I see the woman I love interested and enthralled by an art in which your son is a master—and of which I know hardly the A, B, C. I ask myself if she can care for a creature so inferior as I am—if she can fail to perceive his superiority."

"Jealous, Allan! Oh, I am so sorry. It was I who proposed that they should play duets. It was not Geoffrey's idea. I thought it would encourage Suzette to go on practising. You don't know the delight a pianist feels in accompanying a violin——"

"I think I can imagine it. Suzette takes very kindly to the concertante practice."

"She has improved so much since I first knew her. She has such a talent for music. It never occurred to me that you could object."

"It never occurred to you that I could be a jealous fool. You might just as well say that, for no doubt you think it."

"Yes, I think you are foolish to be jealous. Suzette is as true as steel; and I don't believe Geoffrey has the slightest inclination to fall in love with her."

"Not at this moment, perhaps; but who knows what tender feelings those dulcet strains may bring? However, Suzette will be leaving the neighbourhood, I hope, in a few days."

"Leaving us, you hope!"

"Yes. My mother has written to invite her to Fendyke. She is to see the White Farm, and get acquainted with all our Suffolk neighbours, who declare themselves dying to see her, while I am shooting my father's pheasants."

"You are both going away then? I shall miss you sadly."

"You will have Geoffrey."

"One day out of six, perhaps. He will be hunting or shooting all the rest of the week."

"We shall not be away very long. I don't suppose General Vincent will spare us his daughter for more than a fortnight or three weeks."

"Suzette told me nothing about the invitation."

"She has not received the letter yet. The post had not come in when she left home. I met the postman on my way here, and read my letters as I came along. De Beriot has been too absorbing to allow of my telling Suzette about my mother's letter to me. Shall we go back? Unless that sonata is interminable, it must have come to an end before now."

Mrs. Wornock turned immediately. She saw Allan's uneasiness, and sympathized with him. They went back to the music-room, where there was only silence. Suzette had left the piano, and had put on her hat and jacket. Geoffrey was still standing in front of the music-stand, turning the leaves of the offending sonata.

"Good-bye, dear Mrs. Wornock," said Suzette, kissing her friend. "Now, Allan, I am quite ready."

Allan and Geoffrey shook hands at parting, but not with the usual smiling friendliness.

"How could you be so dreadfully rude, Allan?" Suzette said with a pained voice, as they walked away from the house. "You were quite hateful."

"I know that. I am astounded at my own capacity for hatefulness."

"I shall play no more concertante duets, though I have enjoyed them more than anything in the way of music. It was only the most advanced pupils at the Sacré Cœur who ever had accompanying lessons—and such happiness never fell to my share."

"I should be very sorry to interfere with your—happiness; but I think, Suzette, if you cared for me half as much as I care for you, you would understand how it hurts me to see you so completely in sympathy with another man, and happy with a happiness which I cannot share."

"Why should you not share our happiness, Allan? You are fond of music, I know."

"Fond of music—yes; but I am not a musician. I cannot make music as that young man can. I cannot speak to you as he speaks to you, in that language which is his and yours, and not mine. I am standing outside your world. I feel myself thrust far off from you, while he is so near."

"Allan!" cried Suzette, with a smile that was a pale shadow of her old sportiveness, "can you actually be jealous?"

"I'm afraid I can."

"Jealous about a man who is nothing to me except my dear friend's son. You know how fond I am of Mrs. Wornock—the only real friend I have made since I left the convent—and you ought to understand that I like her son for her sake. And I have been pleased to take my part in the music they both love. But that is all over now. I will not allow myself to be misconstrued by you, Allan. There shall be no more duets."

They were still in Mrs. Wornock's domain, in a wooded drive where the leafless branches overarched the way; and the scene was lonely enough and sheltered enough to allow of Allan taking his sweetheart to his breast and kissing her in a rapture of penitent love.

"My darling, forgive me! If I did not know the pricelessness of my treasure, I should not be so full of unworthy fears. We won't stop the duets for ever, Susie. I must get accustomed to the idea of a gifted wife, who has many talents which I have not. But I hope your musical studies at Discombe may be suspended for a month or so. When you go home, you will find a letter from my mother inviting you to Fendyke. She loves you already, and she wants to know more of you, so that you may really be to her the daughter she has been wishing for ever since I was born. You will go, won't you, Suzette, if the good General will spare you; and I think he will?"

"Are you to be there too?"

"Yes, I am to be there; but you shall not see too much of me. Ours is a shooting county, and I shall be expected to be tramping with my gun nearly every day. I think you will like Fendyke. The house is a fine old house, and the neighbourhood is pretty after a fashion, just as some parts of Holland and Belgium are pretty—sleepy, contented, prosperous, useful."

He walked home with her and stayed to luncheon, so as to secure General Vincent's consent upon the spot. This was obtained without difficulty. The General, having had to dispense with his daughter for at least three-fourths of her existence, was not dependent upon her for society, though he liked to see the bright young face smiling at him across the table at his luncheon and his dinner, and he liked to be played to sleep after dinner, or to have Suzette as a listener when he was in the mood for talking. The greater part of his life was spent out-of-doors—hunting, shooting, fishing, golfing—so that he could afford to be amiable upon this occasion.

"Yes, yes, Suzette, accept the invitation, by all means. The change will do you good. Lady Emily is a most estimable person, and it is only right that you should become better acquainted with her."

"I am very fond of her already," said Suzette. "Then I am really to go, Allan? Lady Emily suggests Saturday—three days from now."

"Well, you are ready, I suppose," said her father. "You have the frocks and things that are necessary."

"Yes, father, I think I have frocks enough; unless you are dreadfully fashionable in Suffolk, Allan."

"The less said about our fashion the better. If you have a stout cloth skirt short enough to keep clear of our mud, that is all you need trouble about. I suppose I shall be allowed to escort Suzette, General?"

"Well, yes, I don't see any objection to your taking care of her on the journey; but I have very lax notions of etiquette. I must ask my sister. Suzie will take her maid, of course; and Suzie's maid is a regular dragon."

Allan walked homeward with a light step and a light heart. The idea of having Suzette as a visitor in his own home, growing every day nearer and dearer to his parents, was rapture. No more concertante duets, no more long-drawn sobbings and sighings on the Stradivarius! He would have his sweetheart all to himself, to pace the level meadow paths, and saunter by the modest river, and loiter by rustic mills and bridges, which Constable may have painted. And in that atmosphere of homely peacefulness he might draw his sweetheart closer to his heart, win her more completely than he had won her yet, and persuade her to consent to a nearer date for their marriage than that far-off summer of the coming year. He counted much on home influences, on his mother's warmhearted affection for the newly adopted daughter.

"A telegram, sir," said the servant who opened the door, startling him from a happy day-dream. "It came nearly an hour ago."

Allan tore open the envelope and glanced carelessly at the message, expecting some trivial communication.

> "Your father is dangerously ill. Come at once. I am writing to postpone Miss Vincent's visit.—Emily Carew."

CHAPTER II
"BEFORE THE NIGHT BE FALLEN ACROSS THY WAY"

A sudden end to a happy day-dream. A hurried preparation and a swift departure. Allan had just time to write to Suzette while his servant was packing a portmanteau and the dog-cart horse was being harnessed for the drive to the station.

He loved his father too well to have room for any selfish thoughts about his own disappointment; but he tried to be hopeful and to think that his mother's alarm had exaggerated the evil, and that the word "dangerously" was rather the expression of her own panic than of the doctor's opinion. It was only natural that she should summon him, the only son, to his father's sick-bed. The illness must be appalling in its suddenness; for in her letter, written on the previous day, she had described him as in his usual health. The suddenness of the attack was in itself enough to scare a woman of Lady Emily's temperament.

Allan telegraphed from Liverpool Street, and was met at the quiet little terminus, where the tiny branch line came to an end on the edge of a meadow, and a hundred yards from a rustic road. The journey to Cambridge had been one of the swiftest, the twenty miles on the branch line of the slowest; a heart-breaking journey for a man whose mind was racked with fears.

It was dark when he arrived; but out of the darkness which surrounded the terminus there came the friendly voice of a groom and the glare of carriage-lamps.

"Ah, is that you, Moyle? Is my father any better?"

His heart sank as he asked the question, with agonizing dread of the reply.

"No, sir; I'm afraid he ain't no better. The doctor from Abbeytown is coming again to-night. Will you drive, sir?"

"No. Get me home as fast as you can, for God's sake!"

"Yes, sir. I brought your old bay mare. She's the fastest we've got."

"Poor old Kitty! Good to the last, is she? Get on."

They were bowling along the level road behind bay Kitty, the first hunter Allan had bought on his own account in his old college days, when his liberal allowance enabled him to indulge his taste in horseflesh. Kitty had distinguished herself in a small way as a steeplechaser before Allan picked her up at Tattersall's, and she was an elderly person when he came into his fortune; so he had left her in the home stables as a general utility horse.

Kitty carried him along the road at a splendid pace, and hardly justified impatience even in the most anxious heart.

His mother was waiting in the porch when he alighted.

"Dear mother," he said, as he kissed and soothed her and led her into the house, "why do you stand out in the cold? You are shivering."

"Not with cold, Allan."

"Poor mother! Is he very ill? Is it really so serious?"

"It could not be more serious, Allan. They thought this morning that he was dying. They told me—to be prepared—for the worst."

The sentence was broken by sobs. She hid her face on her son's breast and sobbed out her grief unchecked by him, only soothed by the gentle pressure of his arm surrounding and, as it were, protecting her from the invincible enemy.

"Doctors are such alarmists, mother; they often take fright too soon."

"Not in this case, Allan; I was with him all through his sufferings. I saw him struggling with death. I knew how near death was in those dreadful hours. It is his heart, Allan. You remember Dr. Arnold's death—how we have cried over the story in Stanley's book. It was like that—sudden, intense suffering. Yesterday he was sitting in his library, placid and at ease among his books. We dined together last night. He was cheerful and full of interesting talk. And this morning at daybreak he was fighting for his life. It was terrible."

"But the danger is past, mother. The struggle is over, please God, and he will be well again."

"Never, never again, Allan. The doctors hold out little hope of that. The awful agony may return at any hour. The mischief is deep seated. We have been living in a fool's paradise. Oh, my dear son, I never knew how fondly I have loved your father till to-day. I thought we should grow old together, go down to the grave hand-in-hand."

"Dear mother, hope for the best. I cannot think—remembering how young a man he seemed the other day at Beechhurst—I cannot think that we are to lose him."

Tears were streaming down Allan's cheeks, tears of which he was unconscious. He dearly loved the father whose mild affection had made his childhood and youth so smooth and easy, the father who had understood every youthful desire, every unexpressed feeling, who in his tenderness and forethought had been as sympathetic as a loving woman.

"Oh, Allan, you will find him aged by ten years since those happy days at Beechhurst. One day of suffering has altered him. It seems as if some invisible writing—the lines of disease and death—had come suddenly out upon his face—lines I never saw till this day."

"Mother, we won't despair. We are passing through the valley of the shadow of death, perhaps—but only passing through. The fight may be hard and bitter; but we shall conquer the enemy; we shall carry our dearest safely over the dark valley. May I see him? I will be very calm and quiet. I am so longing to see him, to hold his dear hand."

"We ought to wait for the doctors, Allan. They both warned me that he must be kept as quiet as possible. He is terribly exhausted. They will be here at eleven o'clock. It might be safer to wait till then."

"Yes, I will wait. Who is with him now?"

"A nurse from the Abbeytown hospital."

"And he is out of pain, and at rest?"

"He was sleeping when I left him—sleeping heavily, worn out with pain, and under the influence of opium."

"Well, we must wait. There is nothing to be done."

Mother and son waited patiently, almost silently, through the slow hours between eight and eleven. They sat together in Lady Emily's morning-room, which was next to the sick man's bedroom. There was a door of communication, and though this was shut, they could hear if there were much movement in the adjoining room.

Lady Emily mooted the question of dinner for the traveller. She urged him to go down to the dining-room and take some kind of meal after his journey; but he shook his head with the first touch of impatience he had shown since his arrival.

"You will wear yourself out, Allan?" she remonstrated.

"No, mother—there is plenty of wear in me. I almost hate myself for being so strong and so full of life while he is lying there——"

Tears ended the sentence.

At last the hands of the clock, which mother and son had both been watching, pointed to eleven, and the hour struck with slow and silvery sound. Then came ten minutes of expectancy, and then the cautious tread of the family practitioner and the consulting physician coming upstairs together.

Allan and his mother went out to the corridor to see them. A few murmured words only, and the two dark figures vanished through the door of the sick-room, and mother and son were alone once more, waiting, waiting with aching hearts and strained ears, that listened for every sound on the other side of the closed door.

The doctors were some time with the patient, and then they went downstairs, and were closeted together in the library for a time that seemed very long to those who waited for the result of their consultation. Those anxious watchers had followed them downstairs, and were standing beside the expiring fire in the hall, waiting as for the voice of fate. The dining-room door was open. A table laid for supper, with glass and silver shining under the lamplight, and the glow of a blazing fire, suggested comfort and good cheer—and seemed to accentuate the gloom in the hearts of the watchers.

What were they talking about, those two in the closed room yonder, Allan wondered. Was their talk all of the sufferer upstairs, and the means of alleviating pain and staving off the inevitable end? or did they wander from that question of life and death to the futilities of everyday conversation—and so lengthen out the agony of those who were waiting for their verdict? At last the door opened, and the two doctors came out into the hall, very grave still, but less gloomy than they had looked in the morning, Lady Emily thought.

"He is better—decidedly better than he was twelve hours ago," said the physician. "We have tided over the immediate peril."

"And he is out of danger?" questioned Allan, eagerly.

"He is out of danger for the moment. He may go on for some time without a recurrence of this morning's attack; but I am bound to tell you that the danger may recur at any time. What has happened must be regarded—I am sorry to be obliged to say it—as the beginning of the end."

There was a silence, broken only by the wife's stifled sobs.

"My God, how sudden it is! and you say it is hopeless?" said Allan, stunned by the sentence of doom.

"To you the thing is sudden; but the mischief is a work of many years. The evil has been there, suspected by your father, but never fully realized.

He consulted me ten years ago, and I gave him the best advice the case allowed—prescribed a regimen which I believe he carefully followed—a regimen which consisted chiefly in quietness and careful living. I told him as much as it was absolutely necessary to tell, taking care not to frighten him."

"You did not tell me that he was a doomed man," Lady Emily said reproachfully.

"My dear lady, to have done that would have been to lessen his chance of cheerful surroundings, to run the risk of sad looks where it was most needful he should find hopefulness. Besides, at that stage of the disease, one might hope for the best—even for a long life, under favourable conditions."

"And now—what is the limit of your hope?" asked Allan.

"I cannot measure the sands in the glass. Another attack like that of to-day would, I fear, be fatal. It is a wonder to me that he survived the agony of this morning."

"And you have told us—that agony may return at any hour. Nothing you can do can prevent its recurrence?"

"I fear not; but we shall do the uttermost."

"May I see him?"

"Not till to-morrow. He is still under the influence of an opiate. Let him rest for to-night undisturbed by one agitating thought. His frame is exhausted by suffering. Mr. Travers will be here again early to-morrow; and if he find his patient as I hope he will find him, then you and Lady Emily can see him for a few minutes. But I must beg that there may be no emotional talk, and that he may be kept very quiet all to-morrow. I will come again early on Saturday."

Mother and son hung upon the physician's words. He was a man whom both trusted, and even in this great strait the idea of other help hardly occurred to either. Yet in the desire to do the uttermost, Allan ventured to say—

"If you would like another opinion, I would telegraph for any one you might suggest—among London specialists."

"A specialist could do nothing more than we have done. The battle is fought and won so far—and when the fight begins again the same weapons will have to be used. The whole college of physicians could do nothing to help us."

And then the doctors went into the dining-room, the physician to fortify himself for a ten-mile drive, the family practitioner to prepare himself for the possibilities of the night. Allan went in with them, at his mother's urgent request, and tried to eat some supper; but his heart was heavy as lead.

He thought of Mrs. Wornock—remembering that pale face looking out of the autumn night, so intense in its searching gaze, the dark grey eyes seeming to devour the face they looked upon—his father sitting unconscious all the while—knowing not how near love was—the romantic love of his younger years, the love which still held all the elements of poetry, the love which had never been vulgarized or out-worn by the fret and jar of daily life.

He would die, perhaps, without ever having seen the face of his early love, without ever having heard the end of her history—die, perhaps, believing that she had given him up easily because she had never really cared for him. The son had felt it in somewise his duty to keep those two apart for his mother's sake; but now at the idea that his father might die without having seen his early love or heard her story from her own lips, it seemed to him that he had acted cruelly and treacherously towards the parent he loved.

There was a further improvement in the patient next morning, and Allan spent the greater part of the day beside his father's bed. There was to be very little conversation; but Allan was told he might read aloud, provided the literature was of an unemotional character. So at his father's request Allan read Chaucer, and the quaint old English verse, with every line of which the patient was familiar, had a soothing and a cheering influence on the tired nerves and brain. There was progress again the day after, and the physician and local watch-dog expressed themselves more than satisfied. The patient might come downstairs on Sunday—might have an airing on the sunniest side of the garden, should there be any sunshine on Monday; but everything was to be done with precautions that too plainly indicated his precarious condition.

"Do you take a more hopeful view than you did the other night?" Allan asked the physician, after the consultation.

"Alas! no. The improvement is greater than I expected; but the substantial facts remain the same. There is deep-seated mischief, which may culminate fatally at any time. I should do wrong to conceal the nature of the case—or its worst possibilities—from you. It is best you should be prepared for the end—for Lady Emily's sake especially, in order that you may lighten the blow for her."

"And the end is likely to come suddenly?"

"Most likely—better perhaps that it should so come. Your father is prepared for death. He is quite conscious of his danger. Better that the end should be sudden—if it spare him pain?"

"Yes, better so. But it is a hard thing. My father is not forty-eight years of age—in the prime of life, with a fine intellect. It is a hard thing."

"Yes, it is hard, very hard. It seems hard even to me, who have seen so many partings. I think you ought to spare your mother as much as you can. Spare her the agony of apprehension; let her have her husband's last days of sunshine and peace. But it is best that you should know. You are a man, and you can suffer and be strong."

"Yes, I can suffer. He seemed so much better this morning. Might he not go on for years, with the care which we shall take of him?"

"He might—but it is scarcely probable."

"We were to have had a young lady visitor here to-day," said Allan, with some hesitation, "the lady who is to be my wife. Her visit has been postponed on account of my father's illness; but I am very anxious that she should know more of my father and mother, and I have been wondering if next week we might venture to have her here. She is very gentle and sympathetic, and I know her society would be pleasant to my father."

"I would not risk it, Mr. Carew, if I were you."

"You think it might be bad for my father?"

"I think it might be hazardous for the young lady. Were a fatal end to come suddenly, you would not like the girl you love to be subjected to the horror of the scene, to be haunted perhaps for years by the memory of that one tragic hour. There is no necessity for her presence here. You can go and see her."

"Yes, and risk being absent in my father's dying hours."

"Better that risk than the risk of her unhappiness, should the end come while she were in the house."

"Yes, I suppose that is so; but I can't help hoping that the end may be far off."

The doctor pressed his hand in silence, and nodded good-bye as he stepped into his carriage. It was not for him to forbid hope, even if he knew that it was a delusive hope.

CHAPTER III
WHILE LEAVES WERE FALLING

Fondly as he loved his betrothed wife, Allan felt that affection and duty alike forbade him to leave his father while the shadow of doom hung over the threshold, while there could be no assurance from day to day that the end would not come before sundown. There had been enough in the physician's manner to crush hopefulness even in the most sanguine breast; and it was in vain that Allan tried to argue within himself against the verdict of learning and experience. He knew in his inmost heart that the physician was right. The ordeal through which George Carew had passed had changed him with the change that too palpably foreshadows the last change of all. In the hollow eyes, the blue-veined forehead and pale lips, in the inert and semi-transparent hands, in the far-off look of the man whose race is run and who has nothing more to do with active life, Allan saw the sign manual of the destroyer. He had need to cherish and garner these quiet days in his father's company, to hang fondly on every word from those pale lips, to treasure each thought as a memory to be hereafter dear and sacred. Whatever other love there might be for him upon this earth—even the love of her whom he had made his second self, upon whom he depended for all future gladness—no claim could prevail against the duty that held him here, by the side of the father whose days were numbered.

"I am so glad to have you with me, Allan," Mr. Carew said, in the grave voice which had lost none of its music, though it had lost much of its power. "It seems selfish on my part to keep you here, away from that nice girl, your sweetheart; but though you are making a sacrifice now— —"

"No, no, no," interrupted Allan, "it is no sacrifice. I had rather be here than anywhere in the world. Thank God that I am here, that no accident of distance has kept me from you."

"Dear boy, you are so good and true—but it is a sacrifice all the same. This is the spring-time of your life, and you ought to be with the girl who makes your sunshine. It is hard for you two to be parted; and I should like her to be here; only this is a house of gloom. God knows what might happen to chill that young heart. It is better that you and I should be alone together, prepared for the worst: and in the days to come, in the far-off days, you will be glad to remember how your love lightened every burden for your dying father."

"Father, my dear father!"

The son uttered words of hope, declared his belief that Heaven would grant the dear patient renewed strength; but the voice in which he spoke the words of cheerfulness was broken by sobs.

"My dear Allan, don't be down-hearted. I am resigned to the worst that can happen. I won't say I am glad that the end is near. That would be base ingratitude to the best of wives, to the dearest of sons, and to Providence which has given me so many good things. This world and this life have been pleasant to me, Allan; and it does seem hard to be called away from such peaceful surroundings, from the home where love is, even though through all that life there has run a dark thread. I think you have known that, Allan. I think that sensitive nature of yours has been conscious of the shadow on my days."

"Yes, I have known that there was a shadow."

"A stronger character would have risen superior to the sorrow that has clouded my life, Allan. I have no doubt that some of the greatest and many of the most useful men the world has known have suffered just such a disappointment as I suffered in my early manhood, and have risen superior to their sorrow. You remember how Austin Caxton counsels his son to live down a disappointed love—how he appeals to the lives of men who have conquered sorrow? 'You thought the wing was broken. Tut, tut, 'twas but a bruised feather.' But in my own case, Allan, the wing *was* broken. I had not the mental stamina, I had not the power of rebound which enables a man to rise superior to the sorrow of his youth. I could not forget my first love. I gave up a year of my life to the search for the girl I loved—who had forsaken me in a foolish spirit of self-sacrifice because she had been told that my marriage with her would be social ruin. She was little more than a child in years—quite a child in ignorance of the world, and of the weight and measure of worldly things. We were both cruelly used, Allan. My mother was a good woman, and a woman who would do nothing which she could not reconcile to her conscience and her own ideas of piety. She acted conscientiously, after her own narrow notions, in bringing about the parting which blighted my youth, and she thought me a wicked son because for two years of my life I held myself aloof from her."

"And in all that time could you find no trace of your lost love?"

"None. I advertised in English and Continental newspapers, veiling my appeal in language which would mean little to the outside world though it would speak plainly to her. I wandered about the Continent—Italy, Switzerland—all along the Rhine, and the Danube, to every place that seemed to offer a chance of success. I had reason to believe that she had been sent abroad, and I thought that her exile would be fixed in some remote district, out of the beaten track. It may be that my research was conducted feebly. I was out of health for the greater part of my wanderings, and I had no one to help me. Another man in my position might have employed a private detective, and might have succeeded where I failed. I was summoned home by the news of my mother's dangerous illness, and I returned remorseful and unhappy. At the thought that she might die unforgiving and unforgiven, my resentment vanished. I recalled all that my mother had been to my childhood and boyhood, and I felt myself an ungrateful son. Thank God, I was home in time to cheer her sick-bed, and to help towards her recovery by the assurance of my unaltered affection. I found that she too had suffered, and I discovered the strength of maternal love under that outward hardness, and allied with those narrow views which had wrecked my happiness. In my gladness at her recovery from a long and dangerous illness, I began to think that the old heart-wound was cured; and when she suggested my marriage with Emily Darnleigh, my amiable playfellow of old, I cheerfully fell in with her views. The union was in every respect suitable, and for me in every respect advantageous. Your mother has been a good and dear wife to me, and never had man less reason to complain against Fate. But there has been the lingering shadow of that old memory, Allan, and you have seen and understood; so it is well you should know all."

Allan tearfully acknowledged the trust confided in him.

"When I am gone, if you care to know the story of my first love, you will find it fully recorded in a manuscript which was written some years ago. Heaven knows what inspired me to go over that old ground, to write of myself almost as I might have written of another man. It was the whim of an idle brain. I felt a strange sad pleasure in recalling every detail of my brief love-story—in conjuring up looks and tones, the very atmosphere of the commonplace surroundings through which my sweet girl and I moved. No touch of romance, no splendour of scenery, no gaiety of racecourse or public garden made the background of our love. A dull London street, a dull

London parlour were all we had for a paradise, and God knows we needed no more. You will smile at a middle-aged man's folly in lingering fondly over the record of his own love-story, instead of projecting himself into the ideal world and weaving a romance of shadows. If I had been a woman, I might have found a diversion for my empty days in writing novels, in every one of which my sweetheart and I would have lived again, and loved and parted again, under various disguises. But I had not the feminine capacity for fiction. It pleased me to write of myself and my love in sober truthfulness. You will read with a mind in touch with mine, Allan; and though you may smile at your father's folly, there will be no scornfulness in your smile."

"My dear, dear father, God knows there will be no smile on these lips of mine if I am to read the story—after our parting. God grant the day for that reading may be far off."

"I will do nothing to hasten it, Allan. Your companionship has renewed my pleasure in life. You can never know how I missed you when this house ceased to be your home. It was different when you were at the University—the short terms, the short distance between here and Cambridge, made parting seem less than parting. But when you transferred yourself to a home of your own, and half a dozen counties divided us, I began to feel that I had lost my only son."

"You had but to summon me."

"I know, I know. But I could not be so selfish as to bring you away from your pleasant surroundings, the prettier country, the more genial climate, your hunting, your falconry, your golf, and your new neighbours. A sick man is a privileged egotist; but even now I feel I am wrong in letting you stay here and lose the best part of the hunting season—to say nothing of that other loss, which, no doubt, you feel more keenly, the loss of your sweetheart's society."

"You need not think about it, father, for I mean to stay. Please regard me as a fixture. If you keep as well next week as you are to-day, I may take a run to Wilts, just to see how Suzette and her father are getting on, and to look round my stable; but I shall be away at most one night."

"Go to-morrow, Allan. I know you are dying to see her."

"Then, perhaps, to-morrow. You really are wonderfully well, are you not?"

"So well that I feel myself an impostor when I am treated as an invalid."

"I may go then; but it will only be to hurry back," said Allan.

His heart beat faster at the thought of an hour with Suzette—an hour in which to look into the frank bright face, to see the truthful eyes looking up at him in all confidence and love, to be assured that three weeks' absence had made no difference, that not the faintest cloud had come between them in their first parting. Yes, he longed to see her, with a lover's heart-sickness. Deeply, tenderly as he treasured every hour of his father's society, he felt that he must steal just as much time from his home duty as would give him one hour with Suzette.

He pored over time-tables, and so planned his journey as to leave Fendyke in the afternoon of one day, and to return in time for luncheon the day after. This was only to be effected by leaving Matcham at daybreak; but a young man who was in the habit of leaving home in the half-light of a September dawn to ride ten miles to a six-o'clock meet was not afraid of an early train.

He caught a fast evening train for Salisbury, and was at Matcham soon after eight. He had written to General Vincent to announce his intention of looking in after dinner, apologizing in advance for so late a visit. His intention was to take a hasty meal, dress, and drive to Marsh House; but at Beechhurst he found a note from the General inviting him to dinner, postponed till nine o'clock on his account; so he made his toilet in the happiest mood, and arrived at Marsh House ten minutes before the hour.

He found Suzette alone in the drawing-room, and had her all to himself for just those ten minutes which he had gained by extra swiftness at his toilet. For half those minutes he had the gentle fluttering creature in his arms, the dark eyes full of tears, the innocent heart all tenderness and sympathy.

"Why would not you let me go to you, Allan?" she remonstrated. "I wanted to be with you and Lady Emily in your trouble. I hope you don't think I am afraid of sickness or sorrow, where those I love are concerned."

"Indeed, dearest, I give you credit for all unselfishness. But I was advised against your visit. The hazard was too awful."

"What hazard, Allan?"

"The possibility of my father's sudden death."

"Oh, Allan, my poor, poor boy! Is it really as bad as that? How sad for you! And you love him so dearly, I know."

"I hardly knew how dearly till this great terror fell upon me. Nothing less than my love for a father whom I must lose too soon—whom I may lose very soon—would have kept me from you so long, Suzette. And now I am only here for a few hours, to see you, to hear you, to hold you in my arms, and to assure myself that there is such a person; to make quite sure that the Suzette who is in my thoughts by day and in all my dreams by night is not a brilliant hallucination—the creature of my mind and fancy."

"I am very real, I assure you—full of human faults."

"I hope you have a stray failing or two lurking somewhere amongst your perfections; but I have not discovered one yet."

"Ah, Allan, Love would not be Love if he could see."

"Tell me all your news, Suzie. What have you been doing with yourself? Your letters have told me a good deal—dear bright letters, coming like a burst of sunshine into my sad life—but they could not tell me enough. I suppose you have been often at Discombe?"

"Yes, I have been there nearly every day. Mrs. Wornock has been ill and depressed. She will not own to being ill, and I could not persuade her to send for the doctor. But I don't think she could be in such low spirits if she were not ill."

"Poor soul!"

"She is so sympathetic, Allan. She has been as keenly interested in your poor father's illness as if he were her dearest friend. She has been so eager to hear about his progress, and has begged me to read the passages in your letters which refer to him. She is so tender-hearted, and enters so fully into other people's sorrows."

"And you have been much with her, and have done all in your power to cheer her, no doubt."

"I have done what I could. We have made music together; but she has not taken her old delight in playing, or in listening to me. She has become dreamy and self-absorbed. I am sure she is out of health."

"And her son, for whose company she was pining all the summer? Has not he been able to cheer her spirits?"

"I hardly know about that. Mr. Wornock is out hunting all day and every day. He has increased his stud since you left, and hunts with three packs of hounds. He comes home after dark, sometimes late for dinner. He and his mother spend the evening together, and no doubt that is her golden hour."

"And has Wornock given up his violin practice?"

"He plays for an hour after dinner sometimes, when he is not too tired?"

"And your musical mornings? Have there been no more of those—no more concertante duets?"

"Allan, I told you that there should be no more such duets for me."

"You might have changed your mind."

"Not after having promised. I considered that a promise."

"Conscientious soul! And you think me a jealous brute, no doubt?"

"I don't think you a brute."

"But a jealous idiot. My dearest, I don't think I am altogether wrong. A wife—or a betrothed wife—should have no absorbing interest outside her husband's or her sweetheart's life; and music is an absorbing interest, a chain of potent strength between two minds. When I heard those impassioned strains on the fiddle, and your tender imitations on the piano, question and answer, question and answer, for ever repeating themselves, and breathing only love— —"

"Oh, Allan, what an ignoramus you are! Do you suppose musical people ever think of anything but the music they are playing?"

"They may not think, but they must feel. They can't help being borne along on that strong current."

"No, no; they have no time to be vapourish or sentimental. They have to be cool and business-like; every iota of one's brain-power is wanted for the notes one is playing, the transitions from key to key—so subtle as to take one by surprise—the changes of time, the syncopated passages which almost take one's breath away— —Hark! there is my aunt. Father asked her in to support me. Uncle Mornington is in London, and she is alone at the Grove."

"I think we could have done without her, Suzie."

Mrs. Mornington's resonant voice was heard in the hall while she was taking off her fur cloak, and the lady appeared a minute later, in a serviceable black-velvet gown, with diamonds twinkling and trembling in her honiton cap, jovial and hearty as usual.

"You poor fellow! I'm very glad to see you," she said, shaking hands with Allan. "I hope your father is better. Of course he is, though, or you wouldn't be here. It's five minutes past nine, Suzie, and as I am accustomed to get my dinner at half-past seven, I hope your cook means to be punctual. Oh, here's my brother, and dinner is announced. Thank goodness!"

General Vincent welcomed his future son-in-law, and the little party went into the cosy dining-room, where Suzette looked her prettiest in the glow of crimson shaded lamps, which flecked her soft white gown and her pretty white neck with rosy lights. Conversation was so bright and cheerful among these four that Allan's thoughts reverted apprehensively now and again to the quiet home in Suffolk and the dark shadow hanging over it. He felt as if there were a kind of treason against family affection in this interlude of happiness, and yet he could not help being happy with Suzette. To-morrow, in the early grey of a winter morning, he would be on his way back to his father.

After dinner Mrs. Mornington established herself in an armchair close to the drawing-room fire, and had so much to say to her brother about Matcham sociology that Allan and his sweetheart, seated by the piano at the other end of the room, were as much alone as if they had been in one of the Discombe copses. No better friend than a piano to lovers who want to be quiet and confidential. Suzette sat before the keyboard and played a few bars now and then, like a running commentary on the conversation.

"You will say all that is kind and nice to Mrs. Wornock for me?" Allan said, after a good deal of other and tenderer talk.

"Yes, I will tell her how kindly you spoke of her; but the best thing I can tell her is that your father is better. She has been so intensely interested about him. I have felt very sorry for her since you went away, Allan."

"Why?"

"Because I cannot help seeing that her son's return has not brought her the happiness she expected. She has been thinking of him and hoping for his coming for years—empty, desolate years, for until she attached herself to you and me she had really no one she cared for. Strange, was it not, that she should take such a fancy to you, and then extend her friendly feeling to me?"

"Yes, it was strange, undoubtedly. But I believe I owe her kindly feeling entirely to my very shadowy likeness to her son."

"No doubt that was the beginning; but I am sure she likes you for your own sake. You are only second to her son in her affection; and I know she is disappointed in her son."

"I hope he is not unkind to her."

"Unkind! No, no, he is kindness itself. His manner to his mother is all that it should be; affectionate, caressing, deferential. But he is such a restless creature, so eager for change and movement. Clever and amiable as he is, there is something wanting in his character; the want of repose, I believe. He hardly ever rests; and there is no rest where he is. He excites his mother, and he doesn't make her happy. Perhaps it is better for her that he is so seldom at home. She is too highly strung to endure his unquiet spirit."

"You like him though, don't you, Suzette, in spite of his faults?"

"Oh, one cannot help liking him. He is so bright and clever; and he has all his mother's amiability; only, like her, he has just a touch of eccentricity—but I hardly like to call it that. A German word expresses it better; he is *überspannt*."

"He is what our American friends call a crank," said Allan, relieved to find his sweetheart could speak so lightly of the man who had caused him his first acquaintance with jealousy.

CHAPTER IV
"LET NO MAN LIVE AS I HAVE LIVED"

Allan went back to Suffolk, and Suzette's life resumed its placid course; a life in which she had for the most part to find her own amusements and occupations. General Vincent was fond and proud of his daughter; but he was not a man to make a companion of a daughter, except at the social board. If Suzette were at home at twelve o'clock to superintend the meal which he called tiffin, and in her place in the drawing-room a quarter of an hour before the eight-o'clock dinner; if she played him to sleep after dinner, or allowed herself to be beaten at chess whenever he fancied an evening game, she fulfilled the whole duty of a daughter as understood by General Vincent. For the rest he had a supreme belief in her high principles and discretion. Her name on the tableau in the parlour at the Sacré Cœur had stood forth conspicuously for all the virtues—order, obedience, propriety, truthfulness. The nuns, who expect perfection in the young human vessel, had discovered no crack or flaw in Suzette.

"She has not only amiability and kindness of heart," said the Reverend Mother, at the parting interview with the pupil's father, "she has plenty of common sense, and she will never give you any trouble."

When the General took his daughter to India, there had been some talk of a companion-governess, or governess-companion, for Suzette; but against this infliction the girl herself protested strongly.

"If I am not old enough or wise enough to take care of myself, I will go back to the convent," she declared. "I would rather take the veil than submit to be governed by a 'Mrs. General.' I had learnt everything the nuns could teach me before I left the Sacré Cœur. I am not going to be taught by an inferior teacher—some smatterer, perhaps. Nobody can teach like the sisters of the Sacré Cœur."

General Vincent had been preached at by his female relatives on this subject of the governess-companion. "Suzette is too young and too pretty to be alone," said one. "Suzette will get into idle habits if there is no one to direct her mind," said another. "A girl's education has only begun when she leaves school," said a third, as gloomy in their foreshadowing of evil as if they had been the three fatal sisters. But the General loved his daughter, and when withdrawing her from the convent had promised her that her life should be happy; so he abandoned an idea that had never been his own.

"A Mrs. General would have been a doosid expensive importation," he told his friends afterwards, "and I knew there would be plenty of nice women to look after Suzie."

Suzette had proved quite capable of looking after herself, unaided by the nice women; indeed, her conduct had been—or should have been—a liberal education to more than one of those nice women, who might have found their matronly exuberances of conversation and behaviour in a manner rebuked by the girl's discretion and self-respect. Suzette passed unsmirched through the furnace of a season at Simla, and a season at Naini Tal, and came to rustic Wiltshire with all the frank gaiety of happy girlhood, and all the *savoir faire* which comes of two years' society experience. She had been courted and wooed, and had blighted the hopes of more than one eligible admirer.

When she came to Matcham, there was again a question of chaperon or companion. The odious word governess was abandoned. But it was said that Indian society was less conventional than English society, and that what might be permitted at Simla could hardly be endured at Wiltshire; and again Suzette threatened to go back to her convent if she were not to be trusted with the conduct of her own life.

"If I cannot take care of myself I am only fit for a cloister," she said. "I would rather be a lay sister, and scrub floors, than be led about by some prim personage, paid to keep watch and ward over me, a hired guardian of my manners and my complexion."

Mrs. Mornington, who was less conventional than the rest of the General's womankind, put in her word for her niece.

"Suzette wants no chaperon while I am living within five minutes' walk," she said. "She can come to me in all her little domestic difficulties; and as for parties, she is not likely to be asked to any ceremonious affair to which I shall not be asked too."

Mrs. Mornington had been as kind and helpful as she had promised to be; and in all domestic cruxes, in all details of home life, in the arrangement of a dinner or the purchase of household goods Suzette had taken counsel with her aunt. The meadows appertaining to the Grove and to Marsh House were conterminous, and a gate had been made in the fence, so that Suzette could run to her aunt at any hour, without hat or gloves, and without showing herself on the high-road.

"If ever we quarrel, that gate will have to be nailed up," said Mrs. Mornington. "It makes a quarrel much more awful when there is a communication of that kind. The walling up of a gate is a public manifesto. If ever we bar each other out, Suzette, all Matcham will know it within twenty-four hours."

Suzette was not afraid that the gate would have to be nailed up. She was fond of her aunt, and fully appreciated that lady's hard-headed qualities; but although she went to her aunt Mornington for advice about the gardener and the cook, the etiquette of invitations and the law of selection with reference to a dinner-party, it was to Mrs. Wornock she went for sympathy in the higher needs of life; it was to Mrs. Wornock she revealed the mysteries of her heart and her imagination.

"I seem to have known you all my life," she told that lady; "and I am never afraid of being troublesome."

"You never can be troublesome," Mrs. Wornock answered, looking at her with admiring affection. "I don't know what I should do without you, Suzette. You and Allan have given my poor worn-out life a new brightness."

"Allan! How fond you are of Allan," Suzette said, musingly. "It seems so strange that you should have taken him to your heart so quickly—only because he is like your son."

"Not only on that account, Suzette. That was the beginning. I am fond of Allan for his own sake. His fine character has endeared him to me."

"You think he has a fine character?"

"Think! I know he has. Surely you know him too, Suzie. You ought to have learnt his value by this time."

"Yes, I know he is good, generous, honest, and true. His love for his father is very beautiful—and yet he found time to come all this way to spend an hour or two with unworthy frivolous me."

"He did not think that a sacrifice, Suzie, for he adores you."

"You really think so—that he cares as much as that?"

"I am very sure that he loves with his whole heart and mind, as his father—may have done before him."

"Oh, his father would have been in earnest, I have no doubt, in any affection; but I doubt if he was ever tremendously in love with Lady Emily. She is all that is sweet and dear in her frank homely way, but not a person to inspire a *grande passion*. Allan's father must have loved and lost in his early youth. There is a shade of melancholy in his voice and manner—nothing at Discombe seemed quite satisfactory to the son and heir. His horses were failures. The hunting was bad—"rotten," Geoffrey called it, but could give no justification for this charge of rottenness. The sport might be good enough for the neighbours in general; but it was not good enough for a man who had run the whole gamut of sport in Bengal, under the best possible conditions. Geoffrey doubted if there was any hunting worth talking about, except in the shires or in Ireland. He thought of going to Ireland directly after Christmas.

"He is bored and unhappy here, Suzette," Mrs. Wornock said one morning, when Suzette found her particularly low-spirited. "The life that suits Allan, and other young men in the neighbourhood, is not good enough for Geoffrey. He has been spoilt by Fortune, perhaps—or it is his sad inheritance. I was an unhappy woman when he was born, and a portion of my sorrow has descended upon my son."

This was the first time she had ever spoken to Suzette of her past life or its sorrows.

"You must not think that, dear Mrs. Wornock. Your son is tired of this humdrum country life, and he'll be all the better and brighter for a change. Let him go to Ireland and hunt. He will be so much the fonder of you when he comes back."

Mrs. Wornock sighed, and began to walk about the room in a restless way.

"Oh, Suzette, Suzette," she said, "I am very unhappy about him! I don't know what will become of us, my son and me. We have all the elements of happiness, and yet we are not happy."

It was a month after the little dinner at Marsh House, and Suzette and her sweetheart had not met since that evening. There had been no change for the better in Mr. Carew's condition; and Allan had felt it impossible to leave the father over whose dwindling hours the shadow of the end was stealing—gently, gradually, inevitably. There were days when all was hushed and still as at the approach of doom—when the head of the household lay silent and exhausted within closed doors, and all Allan could do was to comfort his mother in her aching anxiety. This he did with tenderest thoughtfulness, cheering her, sustaining her, tempting her out into the gardens and meadows, beguiling her to temporary forgetfulness of the sorrow that was so near. There were happier—or seemingly happier—days when the invalid was well enough to sit in his library, among the books which had been his life-companions. In these waning hours he could only handle his books—fondle them, as it were—slowly turning the leaves, reading a paragraph here and there, or pausing to contemplate the outside of a volume, in love with a tasteful binding, the creamy vellum, or gold-diapered back, the painted edges, the devices to which he had given such careful thought in the uneventful years, when collecting and rebinding these books had been the most serious business of his life. He laid down one volume and took up another, capriciously—sometimes with an impatient, sometimes with a regretful, sigh. He could not read more than a page without fatigue. His eyes clouded and his head ached at any sustained exertion. His son kept him company through the grey winter day, in the warm glow of the luxurious room, sheltered by tapestry portières and tall Indian screens. His son fetched and carried for him, between the book-table by the hearth and the shelves that lined the room from floor to ceiling, and filled an ante-room beyond, and overflowed into the corridor.

"My day is done," George Carew said with a sigh. "These books have been my life, Allan, and now I have outlived them. The zest is gone out of them all; and now in these last days I know what a mistake my life has been. Let no man live as I have done, and think that he is wise. A life without variety or action is something less than life. Never envy the student his peaceful meditative days. Be sure that when the end is near he will look back, as I do, and feel that he has wasted his life—yes, even though he leave some monumental work which the world will treasure when he is in the dust—monument more enduring than brass or marble. The man himself, when the shadows darken round him, will know how much he has lost. Life means action, Allan, and variety, and the knowledge of this glorious world into which we are born. The student is a worm and no man. Let no sorrow blight your life as mine has been blighted."

"Dear father, I have always known there was a cloud upon your life—but at least you have made others happy—as husband, father, master——"

"I have not been a domestic tyrant. That is about the best I can say for myself. I have been tolerably indulgent to the kindest of wives. I have loved my only son. Small merits these in a man whose home-life has been cloudless. But I might have done better, Allan. I might have risen superior to that youthful sorrow. I might have taken my dear Emily closer to my heart, travelled over this varied world with her, shown her all that is strangest and fairest under far-off skies instead of letting her vegetate here. I might have gone into Parliament, put my shoulder to the wheel of progress—helped as other men help, with unselfish toil, struggling on hopefully through the great dismal swamp of mistake and muddle-headedness. Better, far better, any life of laborious endeavour, even if futile in result, than the cultured idlers' paradise—better far for me, since in such a life I should have forgotten the past, and might have been a cheerful companion in the present. I chose to feed my morbid fancies; to live the life of retrospection and regret; and now gloomy or dismal—but just that touch of seriousness which tells of deep thoughts. He is a most interesting man. I wish you could have seen him while he was at Beechhurst. I fear he will never leave Fendyke again."

Mrs. Wornock sighed and sat silent, while Suzette went to the piano and played a short fugue by their favourite Sebastian Bach—played with tender touch, lengthening out every slow passage in her pensive reverie.

There had been no more concertante duets. Geoffrey had entreated her to go on with their mutual study of De Beriot and the older composers, Corelli, Tartini, and the rest; but she had obstinately refused.

"The music is difficult and tiring," she said.

This was her first excuse.

"We will play simpler music—the lightest we can find. There are plenty of easy ducts."

"Please don't think me capricious if I confess that I don't care about playing with the violin. It takes too much out of one. I am too anxious."

"Why should you be anxious? I am not going to be angry or disagreeable at your *brioches*—should you make any."

She still refused, lightly but persistently; and he saw that she had made up her mind.

"I begin to understand," he said, with an offended air; and there was never any further talk of Suzette as an accompanist.

Geoffrey was seldom at home in the daytime after this refusal, and life at the Manor dropped back into the old groove. Mrs. Wornock and Suzette spent some hours of every day together; and, now that the weather often made the garden impossible, the organ and piano afforded their chief occupation and amusement. Suzette was enthusiastic, and pleased with her own improvement under her friend's guidance. It was not so much tuition as sympathy which the elder woman gave to the younger. Suzette's musical talent, since she left her convent, had been withering in an atmosphere of chilling indifference. Her father liked to be played to sleep after dinner; but he hardly knew one air from another, and he called everything his daughter played Rubinstein.

"Wonderful fellow that Rubinstein!" he used to say. "There seems no end to his compositions; and, to my notion, they've only one fault—they're all alike."

Suzette heard of Geoffrey, though she rarely saw him. His mother talked of him daily; but there was a regretful tone in all her talk. Nothing that the end has come, I begin to understand what a contemptible creature I have been."

"Contemptible! My dear father, if every student were so to upbraid himself after a life of plain living and high thinking, such as you have led——"

"Plain living and high thinking are of very little good, Allan, if they result in no useful work. Plain living and high thinking may be only a polite synonym for selfish sloth."

"Father, I will not hear you depreciate yourself."

"My dear son! It is something to have won your love."

"And my mother. Is it not something to have made her happy?"

"For that I must thank her own sweet disposition. My reproach is that I might have made her happier. I have wronged her by brooding over an old sorrow."

"She has not been jealous of the love that came before you belonged to her. She loves and honours you."

"Far beyond my merits. Providence has been very good to me, Allan."

There was a silence. More books were asked for and brought, languidly opened, languidly closed, and laid aside. Yes, the zest had gone out of them. The languor of excessive weakness can find no beauty even in things most beautiful.

CHAPTER V
"CHANCE CANNOT CHANGE MY LOVE, NOR TIME IMPAIR"

Suzette endured her lover's absence with a philosophical cheerfulness which somewhat surprised her aunt.

"Upon my word, Suzie, I am half inclined to think that you don't care a straw for Allan," Mrs. Mornington exclaimed one day, when her niece came singing across the wintry lawn, crisp under her footsteps after the morning frost.

Suzette looked angrier than her aunt had ever seen her look till this moment.

"Auntie, how can you say anything so horrid? Not care for Allan! When he is in sad trouble, too! This morning's letter gives a most melancholy account of his father. I fear the end must be near. It was horrid of me to come running and singing over the grass; but these frosty mornings are so delicious. Look at that glorious blue sky!"

"And when all is over, Allan will come back to you, I suppose? I must say you have endured the separation in the calmest way."

"Why should I make myself unhappy? I know that it is Allan's duty to be at Fendyke. The only thing I regret is that I can't be there too, to help him to bear his sorrow."

"And you do not mind being parted from him. You can live without him?"

Suzette smiled at the sentimental question from the lips of her practical aunt, whose ideas seemed rarely to soar above the daily cares of housekeeping and the considerations of twopence as against twopence halfpenny.

"I have had to live without him over twenty years, auntie."

"Yes, but I thought that the moment a girl was engaged she found life impossible in the absence of her sweetheart."

"I think that kind of girl must be very empty-headed."

"And your little brains are well furnished—and then you have Mrs. Wornock and her son to fill up your days," said Mrs. Mornington, with a searching look.

"I have Mrs. Wornock, and I like her society. I see very little of Mrs. Wornock's son."

"Where is he, then? I thought he was at the Manor."

"He is seldom at home in the daytime, and I am never there in the evening."

"And so you never meet. You are like Box and Cox. So much the more satisfactory for Allan, I should say."

"Really, aunt, you are in a most provoking mood this morning. I'm afraid the butcher's book must be heavier than you like."

It was Tuesday—Mrs. Mornington's terrible day—the day on which the tradesmen's books came up for judgment; a day on which the cook trembled, and even the housemaids felt the electricity in the atmosphere.

"I never like the butcher's book," said the lady; "but that isn't what set me thinking about you and Allan. I have been thinking about you for ever so long. I'm afraid you are not so fond of him as you ought to be."

"Auntie, you have no right to say that."

"Why not, pray, miss?"

"Because, perhaps, if you had not urged me to accept him, I might not have said 'Yes' when he asked me the second time. Oh, pray don't look so frightened. I am very fond of him—very fond of him. I know that he is good and true and kind, and that he loves me better than I deserve to be loved, and thinks me better than I am—cleverer, prettier, altogether superior to my work-a-day self. And it is very sweet to have a lover who thinks of one in that exalted way. But I am not romantically in love, auntie. I don't believe that it is in my nature to be romantic. I see the bright and happy side of life. I see things to laugh at. I am not sentimental."

"Well, I dare say Allan can get on without sentiment, so long as he knows you like him better than anybody else in the world; and now, as there is no reason whatever for delay, the sooner you marry him the better."

"I am afraid he will lose his father before long, auntie; and then he can't marry for at least a year."

"Nonsense, child. He won't be a widow. I dare say Lady Emily will be marrying when the year is out. Three months will be quite long enough for Allan to wait. You can make the wedding as quiet as you like."

Suzette did not prolong the argument. The subject was too remote to need discussion. Mrs. Mornington went back to her tradesmen's books, and Suzette left her absorbed in the calculation of legs and sirloins, and the deeper mysteries of soup meat and gravy beef.

Christmas had come and gone, a very tranquil season at Matcham, marked only by the decoration of the church and the new bonnets in the tradespeople's pews. It was a dull, grey day at the end of the year, the last day but one, and Suzette was walking home in the early dusk after what she called a long morning with Mrs. Wornock, a long morning which generally lasted till late in the afternoon. But these mid-winter days were too short to allow of Suzette walking home alone after tea; so unless her own or her aunt's pony-carriage were coming for her, she left the Manor before dusk.

To-day Mrs. Wornock had been sadder even than her wont, as if saddened by the last news from Fendyke, and sorrowing for Allan's loss; so Suzette had stayed longer than usual, and as she walked homeward the shadows of evening began to fall darkly, and the leafless woods looked black against the faint saffron of the western sky. The sun had shown himself, as if reluctantly, an hour before his setting.

Presently in the stillness she heard horses' hoofs walking slowly on the moist road, and the next turn in the path showed her Geoffrey Wornock, in his red coat, leading his horse.

It was the first time they had met since her refusal to play any more duets with him, and, without knowing why, she felt considerable embarrassment at the meeting, and was sorry when he stopped to shake hands with her, stopped as if he meant to enter into conversation.

"Going home alone in the dark, Miss Vincent?"

"Yes; the darkness comes upon one unawares in these short winter days. I stayed with Mrs. Wornock because she seemed out of spirits. I am glad you are home early to cheer her."

"That is tantamount to saying you are glad I have lamed my horse. I should be on the other side of Andover, in one of the best runs of the season, if it were not for that fact. When one is thrown out, the run is always quite the best—or so one's friends tell one afterwards."

"I am sorry for your horse. I hope he isn't much hurt?"

"I don't know. Lameness in a horse is generally an impenetrable mystery. One only knows that he is lame. The stable will find half a dozen theories to account for it, and the vet will find a seventh, and very likely they may all be wrong. I'll walk with you to the high-road at least."

"And give the poor horse extra work. Not for the world!"

"Then I'll take him on till I am within halloo of the stables, and then come back to you, if you'll walk on very slowly."

"Pray don't! I am not at all afraid of the dusk."

"Please walk slowly," he answered, looking back at her and hurrying on with his horse.

Suzette was vexed at his persistence; but she did not want to be rude to him, were it only for his mother's sake. How much better it would have been had he gone straight home to cheer that fond mother by his company, instead of wasting his time by walking to Matcham, as he would perhaps insist upon doing.

He looked white and haggard, Suzette thought; but that might only be the effect of the evening light, or it might be that he was tired after a laborious day. She had not much time to think about him. His footsteps sounded on the road behind her. He was running to overtake her. It occurred to her that she might turn this persistence of his to good account. She might talk to him about his mother, and urge him to spend a little more of his time at home, and do a little more to brighten that lonely life.

"I met one of the lads," he said, "and got rid of that poor brute."

"I am so sorry you should think it necessary to come with me."

"You mean you are sorry that I should snatch a brief and perilous joy—half an hour in your company—after having abstained from pleasure and peril so long."

"If you are going to talk nonsense, I shall go back to the house and ask your mother to send me home in her brougham."

"Then I won't talk nonsense. I don't want to offend you; and you are so easily offended. Something offended you in our duets. What was it, I wonder? Some ignorant sin of mine? some passage played *troppo appassionato*? some *cantabile* phrase that sounded like a sigh from an over-laden heart! Did the music speak too plainly, Suzette?"

"This is too bad of you!" exclaimed Suzette, pale with anger. "You take a mean advantage of finding me alone here. I won't walk another step with you!"

She turned and walked quickly in the opposite direction as she spoke; but she was some distance from the house, at least ten minutes' walk, and her heart sank at the thought of how much Geoffrey Wornock could say to her in ten minutes. Her heart was beating violently, louder and faster than she had ever felt it beat. Did it matter so much what nonsense he might talk to her—idle breath from idle lips? Yes, it seemed to her to matter very much. She would be guilty of unpardonable treason to Allan if she let this man talk. It seemed to her as if these wild words of his—mere rodomontade—made an epoch in her life.

He seized her by the arm with passionate vehemence, but not roughly.

"Suzette! Suzette! you must—you shall hear me!" he said. "Go which way you will, I go with you. I did not mean to speak. I have tried—honestly—to avoid you. Short of leaving this place altogether, I have done my uttermost. But Fate meant us to meet, you see. Fate lamed my horse—the soundest hunter of them all. Fate sent you by this lonely path at the nick of time. You shall hear me! Say what you like to me when you have heard. Be as hard, as cruel, as constant to your affianced lover as you please; but you shall know that you have another lover—a lover who has been silent till to-night, but who loves you with a love which is his doom. Who says that about love and doom? Shakespeare or Tennyson, I suppose. Those two fellows have said everything."

"Mr. Wornock, you are very cruel," she faltered. "You know how sincerely I am attached to your mother, and that I wouldn't for the world do anything to wound her feelings, but you are making it impossible for me ever to enter her house again."

"Why impossible? You are trembling, Suzette. Oh, my love! my dear, dear girl, you tremble at my touch. My words go home to your heart. Suzette, that other man has not all your heart. If he had, you would not have been afraid to go on with our music. If your heart was his, Orpheus himself could not have moved you."

"I was not afraid. You are talking nonsense. I left off playing because Allan did not like to see me absorbed in an occupation which he could not share. It was my duty to defer to his opinion."

"Yes, he heard, he understood. He knew that my heart was going out to you—my longing, passionate heart. He could read my mystery, though you could not. Suzette, is it hopeless for me? Is he verily and indeed the chosen? Or do you care for him only because he came to you first—when you knew not what love means? You gave yourself lightly, because he is what people call a good fellow. He cannot love you as I love you, Suzette. Love is something less than all the world for him. No duty beside a father's sick-bed would keep me from my dearest, if she were mine. I would be your slave. I could live upon one kind word a month, if only I might be near you, to behold and adore."

He had released her arm, but he was walking close by her side, still in the direction of the Manor House, she hurrying impetuously, trying to conquer her agitation, trying to make light of his foolishness, and yet deeply moved.

"You are very unkind," she said at last, with a piteousness that was like the complaint of a child.

"Unkind! I am a miserable wretch pleading for life, and you call me unkind. Suzette, have pity on me! I have not succumbed without a struggle. I loved you from the hour we met—from that first hour when my heart leapt into a new life at the sound of your voice. On looking back, it seems to me now that I must have so loved you from the beginning. I can recall no hour in which I did not love you. But I have fought the good fight, Suzette. Self-banished from the presence I adore, I have lived between earth and sky, until, though I have something of the sportsman's instinct, I have come almost to hate the music of the hounds and the call of the huntsman's horn, because in every mile my horse galloped he was carrying me further from you, and every hour I spent far afield was an hour I might have spent with you."

"It is cruel of you to persecute me like this."

"No, no, Suzette; you must not talk of persecution. If I am rough and vehement to-night, it is because I am resolute to ask the question that has been burning on my lips ever since I knew you. I will not be put off from that. But once the question asked and answered I have done, and, if it must be so, you have done with me. There shall be no such thing as persecution. I am here at your side, your devoted lover—no better man than Allan Carew, but I think as good a man, with as fair a record, of as old and honourable a race, richer in this world's gear; but that's not much to such a woman as Suzette. It is for you to choose between us; and it is not because you said yes to him before you had ever seen my face that you are to say no to me, if there is the faintest whisper in your heart that pleads for me against him."

She stood silent, her eyelids drooping over eyes that were not tearless. His words thrilled her, as his violin had thrilled her sometimes in some lingering, plaintive passage of old-world music. His face was near hers, and his hand was on her shoulder, detaining her.

The intellectuality, the refinement of the delicately chiselled features, the pallor of the clear complexion were intensified by the dim light. She could not but feel the charm of his manner.

He was like Allan—yet how unlike! There was a fascination in this face, a music in this voice, which were wanting in Allan, frank, and bright, and honest, and true though he was. There was in this man just the element of poetry and unreasoning impulse which influences a woman in her first youth more than all the manly virtues that ever went to the making of the Christian Hero.

Suzette had time to feel the power of that personal charm before she collected herself sufficiently to answer him with becoming firmness. For some moments she was silent, under the influence of a spell which she knew must be fatal to her peace and Allan's happiness, should she weakly yield. No, she would not be so poor, so fickle a creature. She would be staunch and true, worthy of Allan's love and of her father's confidence.

"Why, if I were to palter with the situation," she thought—"if I were to play fast and loose with Allan, my father might think he had been mistaken in trusting me without a chaperon. He would never respect me or believe in me again. And Allan? What could Allan think of me were I capable of jilting him?"

Her heart turned cold at the idea of his indignation, his grief, his disgust at a woman's perfidy.

She conquered her agitation with an effort, and answered her daring lover as lightly as she could. She did not want Geoffrey to know how he had shaken her nerves by his vehement appeal.

She knew now, standing by his side, with that eloquent face so near her own, that musical voice pleading to her—she knew how often his image had been present to her thoughts at Discombe Manor, while he himself was away.

"It is very foolish of you to waste such big words upon another man's sweetheart," she said. "Pray believe that when I accepted Allan Carew as my future husband, I accepted him once and for ever. There was no question of seeing some one else a little later, and liking some one else a little better.

There may be girls who do that sort of thing; but I should be sorry that anybody could think me capable of such inconstancy. Allan Carew and I belong to each other for the rest of our lives."

"Is that a final answer, Miss Vincent?"

"Absolutely final."

"Then I can say no more, except to ask your forgiveness for having said too much already. If you will go on to the house, and talk to my mother for a few minutes, I'll go to the stables and order the brougham to take you home. It is too dark for you to walk home alone."

There was no occasion for the brougham. A pair of lamps in the drive announced the arrival of Miss Vincent's pony-cart, which had been sent to fetch her.

CHAPTER VI
AT EVENSONG

The windows were darkened at Fendyke. The passing bell had tolled the years of the life that was done, sounding solemnly and slowly across the level fields, the deep narrow river, the mill-streams and pine-woods, the scattered hamlets lying far apart on the great flat, where the sunsets linger late and long. All was over, and Allan had to put aside his own sorrow in order to comfort his mother, who was heart-broken at the loss of a husband she had idolized, with a love so quiet and unobtrusive, so little given to sentimental utterances, that it might have been mistaken for indifference.

She wandered about the darkened house like some lost soul in the dim under-world, unable to think of anything, or to speak of anything but her loss. She looked to Allan for everything, asserted her authority in no detail.

"Let all be as he wished," she said to her son. "Let us think only of pleasing him. You know what he would like, Allan. You were with him so much towards the last. He talked to you so freely. Think only of him, and of his wishes."

She could not divest herself of the idea that her husband was looking on at all that happened, that this or that arrangement might be displeasing to him. She was sure that he would wish the sternest simplicity as to the funeral. His own farm-labourers were to carry him to his grave, and the burial was to be at dusk. He had himself prescribed those two conditions. He wished to be laid in his grave at set of sun, when the hireling's daily toil was over, and the humblest of his neighbours could have leisure to follow him to his last bed. And then he had quoted Parson Hawker's touching lines:—

"Sunset should be the time, they said,
To close their brother's narrow bed.
'Tis at that pleasant hour of day
The labourer treads his homeward way;
His work is o'er, his toil is done,

And therefore at the set of sun,
To wait the wages of the dead,
We lay our hireling in his bed."

Those lines were written for the tillers of the earth; but George Carew's thoughts of himself were as humble as if he had been the lowest of day labourers. Indeed, in those closing hours of life, when the record of a man's existence is suddenly spread out before him like the scroll which the prophet laid before the king, there is much in that comprehensive survey to humiliate the proudest of God's servants, much which makes him who has laboured strenuously despair at the insufficiency of the result, the unprofitableness of his labour. How, then, could such a man as George Carew fail to perceive his unworthiness?—a man who had let life go by him, who had done nothing, save by a careless automatic beneficence, to help or better his fellow-men, to whom duty had been an empty word, and the Christian religion a lifeless formula.

The Squire of Fendyke was laid to rest in the pale twilight of early March, the winter birds sounding their melancholy evensong as the coffin was lowered into the grave. The widow and her son stood side by side, with those humbler neighbours and dependents clustering round them. No one had been bidden to the funeral, no hour had been named, and the gentry of the district, whose houses lay somewhat wide apart, knew nothing of the arrangements till afterwards. There were no empty carriages to testify to the decent grief which stays at home, while liveried servants offer the tribute of solemn faces and black gloves. Side by side, Lady Emily and her son walked through the grounds of Fendyke to the churchyard adjoining. The wintry darkness had fallen gently on those humble graves when the last "Amen" had been spoken, and mother and son turned slowly and sadly towards the desolate home.

Allan stayed in his mother's sitting-room till after midnight, talking of their dead. Lady Emily found a sad pleasure in talking of the husband she had lost, in dwelling fondly upon his virtues, his calm and studious life, his non-interference with her household arrangements, his perfect contentment with the things that satisfied her.

"There never was a better husband, Allan," she said, with a tearful sigh, "and yet I know I was not his first love."

"Not his first love. Alas! no, poor soul," mused Allan, when he had bidden his mother good night, and was seated alone in front of his father's bureau, alone in the dead middle of the night, steeped in the concentrated light of the large shaded lamp, while all the rest of the room was in semi-darkness.

"Not his first love! Poor mother. It is happy for you that you know not how near that first love was to being the last and only love of your husband's life. Thank God, you did not know."

Often in those quiet days while his father was gradually fading out of life, Allan had argued with himself as to whether it was or was not his duty to reveal Mrs. Wornock's identity with the woman to whom George Carew had dedicated a lifetime of regret, and so to give his father the option of summoning that sad ghost out of the past, of clasping once again the vanished hand, and hearing the voice that had so long been unheard. There would have been rapture, perhaps, to the dying man in one brief hour of re-union; but that hour could not give back youth, or youthful dreams. There would have been the irony of fate in a meeting on the brink of the grave; and whatever touch of feverish gladness there might have been for the dying in that brief hour, its after consequences would have been full of evil for the mourning wife. Better, infinitely better, that she should never know the romance of her husband's youth, never be able to identify the woman he loved, or to inflict upon her own tender heart the self-torture of comparison with such a woman as Mrs. Wornock.

For Lady Emily, in her happy ignorance of all details, that early love was but a vague memory of a remote past, a memory too shadowy to be the cause of retrospective jealousy. She knew that her husband had loved and sorrowed; and she knew no more. It must needs be painful to her to identify his lost love in the person of a lady whom her son valued as a friend, and to whom her son's future wife was warmly attached. Allan had felt therefore that he was fully justified in leaving Mrs. Wornock's story unrevealed, even though by that silence he deprived the man who had loved her of the last tearful farewell, the final touch of hands that had long been parted.

He was full of sadness to-night as he turned the key in the lock, and lifted the heavy lid of the bureau at which he had so often seen his father seated, arranging letters and papers with neat, leisurely hands, and the pensive placidity which characterized all the details of his life. That bureau was the one repository for all papers of a private nature, the one spot peculiarly associated with him whom they had laid in the grave at evensong. No one else had ever written on that desk, or possessed the keys of those quaintly inlaid drawers.

And now the secrets of the dead were at the mercy of the survivors, so far as he had left any trace of them among those neatly docketted papers, those packets of letters folded and tied with red tape, or packed in large envelopes, sealed, and labelled.

Allan touched those packets with reverent hands, glanced at their endorsement, and replaced them in the drawers or pigeon-holes as he had found them. He was looking for the manuscript of which his father had told him; the story of "a love which never found its earthly close."

Yes, it was here, under his hand; a thin octavo, bound in limp morocco, a manuscript of something less than a hundred pages, in the hand he knew so well, the small, neat hand that, to Allan's fancy, told of the leisurely life, the mind free from fever and fret, the heart that beat in slow time, and had long outlived the quick alternations of passionate feeling. Allan drew his chair nearer the lamp, and began to read.

CHAPTER VII
"THE DEAD MAN TOUCH'D ME FROM THE PAST"

"I wonder how many lives there are like mine in this prosperous England of ours, eminently respectable, comfortable, and altogether protected from the worst hazards of fate, happy even, according to the standard measure of happiness among the squirearchy of England—and yet cold and colourless. I wonder how many men there are in every generation who drift along the slow current of a sluggish river, and who call that monotonous progress living. Up the river with the rising tide; down the river with the ebbing tide; up and down, to and fro, between level banks that are always the same, with never a hill and never a crag to break the monotony of the outlook.

"We have a river within a stone's throw of my gates which always seems to me the outward and visible sign of my inward and spiritual life, a river that flows past farms and villages, and for any variety of curve or accident of beauty might just as well be a canal—a useful river bearing the laden barges down to the sea, a river on which a pleasure-boat is as rare as a kingfisher on its banks. And so much might be said of my life; a useful life within the everyday limits of English morality; but a life that nobody will remember or regret, outside my own household, when I am gone.

"This is no complaint that I am writing, to be read when I am in my grave by the son I hope to leave behind me. Far be such a thought from me the writer, and from him the reader. It is only a statement, a history of a youthful experience which has influenced my mature years, chiefly because on that boyish romance I spent all the stock of passionate feeling with which nature had endowed me. It was not much, perhaps, in the beginning. I was no Byronic hero. I was only an impulsive and somewhat sentimental youth, ready to fall in love with the first interesting girl I met, but not to find my Egeria among the audience at a music-hall, or in a dancing garden.

"Do not mistake me, Allan. I have loved your mother truly and even warmly, but never romantically. All that constitutes the poetry, the romance of love, the fond enthusiasm of the lover, vanished out of my life before I was three and twenty. All that came afterwards was plain prose.

"It was in the second year of my university life, and towards the end of the long vacation, that I allowed myself to be persuaded to attend a *séance* to be given by some so-called spiritualists in the neighbourhood of Russell Square. Mr. Home, the spiritualist, had been frightening and astonishing people by certain unexplainable manifestations, and he had been lucky enough to number among his patrons and disciples such men as Bulwer Lytton, William and Robert Chambers, and others of almost equal distinction. To the common herd it seemed that, there must be some value in manifestations which could interest and even convince these superior intellects; so, with the prestige of Home's performances, and with an article in the *Cornhill Magazine* to assist them, the people near Russell Square were doing very good business.

"Twice, and sometimes three times a week, they gave a *séance*, and though they did not take money at the doors, or advertise their entertainment in the daily papers, they had their regular subscribers among the faithful, and these subscribers could dispose of tickets of admission among the common herd. As two of the common herd, Gerald Standish and I got our tickets from Mrs. Ravenshaw, a literary lady of Gerald's acquaintance, who had written a spiritualistic novel, and was a profound believer in all the spiritualistic phenomena. Her vivid description of the dark *séance* and its wonders had aroused Gerald's curiosity, and he insisted that I, who was known among the men of my year as a favourite pupil of the then famous mathematical coach, should go with him and bring the severe laws of pure science to bear upon the spirit world.

"I was incurious and indifferent, but Gerald Standish was a genius, and my particular chum. I could not, therefore, be so churlish as to refuse so slight a concession. We dined together at the Horseshoe Restaurant, then in the bloom of novelty; and, after a very temperate dinner, we walked through the autumn dusk to the quiet street on the eastward side of Russell Square, where the priest and priestess of the spirit-world had set up their temple.

"The approach of the mysteries was sadly commonplace, a shabby hall door, an airless passage that smelt of dinner, and for the temple itself a front parlour sparsely furnished with the most Philistine of furniture. When we entered, the room was empty of humanity. An oil-lamp on a cheffonier by the fireplace dimly lighted the all-pervading shabbiness. The scanty moreen curtains—lodging-house curtains of the poorest type—were drawn. The furniture consisted of a dozen or so of heavily made mahogany chairs with horse-hair cushions, a large round table on a massive pedestal, supported on three clumsily carved claws, and a bookcase against the wall facing the windows, or I should say rather a piece of furniture which might be supposed to contain books, as the contents were hidden by a brass lattice-work lined with faded green silk. The gloom of the scene was inexpressible, and seemed accentuated by a dismal street cry which rose and fell ever and anon from the distance of Hunter or Coram Street.

"'We are the first,' Gerald whispered, a fact of which I did not require to be informed, and for which he ought to have apologized, seeing that he had deprived me of my after-dinner coffee, and dragged me off yawning, full of alarm lest we should be late.

"Gradually, and in dismal silence, diversified only by occasional whisperings, about a dozen people assembled in the dimness of the dreary room. Among them came Mrs. Ravenshaw and her jovial, business-like husband, who seated themselves next Gerald and me, and confided their experiences of past *séances*. The lady was full of faith and enthusiasm. The gentleman was beginning to have doubts. He had heard things from unbelievers which had somewhat unsettled him. He had invested a good many half-guineas in this dismal form of entertainment, and had wasted a good deal of time in bringing his gifted wife all the way from Shooter's Hill, and, so far, they had got no forwarder than on the first *séance*. They had seen strange things. They had felt the ghastly touch of hands that seemed like dead hands, and which ordinary people would run a mile to avoid. That heavy mahogany table had shuddered and thrilled under the touch of meeting hands; had lifted itself like a rearing horse; had throbbed out messages purporting to come from the dead. Strange sounds had been in the air; angelic singing, as of souls in Elysium; and some among the audience had gone away after each *séance* touched and satisfied, believing themselves upon the threshold of other worlds, feeling their commonplace lives shone upon by supernal light, content henceforward to dwell upon this dull cold earth, since they were now assured of a link between earth and heaven.

"Mrs. Ravenshaw, as became an imaginative writer, was of this idealistic temperament, receptive, confiding; but her husband was a man of business, and wanted to see value for his money. He explained his views to me in a confidential voice while we waited. 'Yes, they had undoubtedly seen and heard strange things. They had seen bodies—living human bodies—floating in the air—yes, floating in the frowsy atmosphere of this shabby parlour, atmosphere which it were base flattery to call "air." They had enjoyed this abnormal experience; but, after all, how is the cause of humanity, or the march of enlightenment to be advantaged by the flotation of an exceptional subject here and there? If everybody could float, well and good. The gain would be immense, except for boot-makers and chiropodists, who must suffer for the general weal. But for mediumistic persons, at the rate of one per million of the population, to be carried by viewless powers on the empty air was of the smallest practical use. An improvement in the construction of balloons would be infinitely more valuable.'

"We waited nearly an hour in all—we had arrived half an hour before the stated opening of the *séance*, and we waited five and twenty minutes more, and were yawning and fidgeting hopelessly before the door opened, and a dismal-looking man with a pallid face and long hair, came into the room, followed by a slovenly woman in black, with bare arms, and a towzled, highly artistic flaxen head. He bowed solemnly to the assembled company, looked from the company to the woman, and murmured in a sepulchral voice, 'My wife,' by way of general introduction.

"The flaxen-headed lady seated herself at the large round table, and the dark-haired vampire-like man crept about the room inviting his audience to take their places at the same mystic table. We formed a circle, hand touching hand, the long-haired professor on one side of the table, the flaxen wife on the other. Gerald and I were separated by the width of the table, and the enthusiastic novelist and her practical husband were also as far apart as circumstances would permit.

"My next neighbour on the right was a tall, burly man with a strong North of Ireland accent, a captain in the mercantile marine, Mrs. Ravenshaw informed me. The people who met in this dreary room had come by some knowledge of one another's social status and opinions, although conversation was sternly discouraged as offensive to the impalpable company we were there to cultivate. A gloomy silence, and a vaguely uncomfortable expectancy of something ghastly were the prevailing characteristics of the assembly.

"Mrs. Ravenshaw had informed me that the seaman on my right was an unbeliever, and that he courted the spirits only with the malicious desire of doing them a bad turn. There had been the premonitory symptoms of a row on more than one occasion, and he had been the source and centre of the adverse feeling which had shown itself at those times.

"My left-hand neighbour was an elderly woman in black, who looked like a spinster, and who, instead of the bonnet of everyday life, wore a rusty Spanish mantilla, and a black velvet band across her high narrow forehead, confining braids of chestnut hair whose artificial origin was patent to every eye. As the *séance* progressed she frequently shed tears. Mrs. Ravenshaw, who was in her confidence, whispered to me that this lady came there to hold mystic converse with an officer in the East-India Company's Service, to whom she had been betrothed thirty years before, and who had died in Bengal, after marrying the daughter of a native money-lender and an English governess. It comforted his devoted sweetheart to hear from his own lips, as it were, that he had led a wretched existence with his half-caste wife, and had never ceased to repent his inconstancy to his dearest Amanda. Amanda was the name of the lady in the mantilla, Amanda Jones. It amuses me to recall these details, to dwell upon the opening of a scene which I entered upon so casually, and which was to exercise so lasting an influence upon my life.

"The *séance* proceeded after the vulgar routine of such mysteries in England and in America. We sat in the frowzy darkness, and heard each other's breathing as we listened to the mysterious rappings, now here, now there, now high, now low, as of some sportive dressmaker rapping her thimbled finger on table, or shutter, or ceiling, or wall. We heard strange messages thumped out, or throbbed out by the excitable mahogany, which became more and more vehement, as if the beating of our hearts, the swift current of blood in all our arteries were being gradually absorbed by that vitalised wood. The German woman translated the rappings into strange scraps of speech, which for some of the audience were full of meaning—private communications from friends long dead, allusions to the past, which were sometimes received in blank wonder, sometimes welcomed as proof irresistible of thought-transference between the dead and the living. The mighty dead, with names familiar to us all, condescended to hold communion with us. Spinosa, Bacon, Shelley, Sir John Franklin, Mesmer—a strange mixture of personalities—but, alas! the feebleness of their communications gave a crushing blow to the theory of a progressive existence beyond the grave.

"'I should like to know how it's done,' said the sea-captain, suddenly, in an aggressive voice, which irreverent interruption the professor and some of the audience rebuked by an indignant hush.

"The whole business wearied me. I was moved to melancholy rather than to laughter as I realized the depth of human credulity which was indicated by the hushed expectancy of the dozen or so of people sitting round a table in the dark in a shabby Bloomsbury lodging-house, and expecting communications from the world after death—the inexplicable shadow-land of which to think is to enter into the regions of all that is most serious and solemn in human thought—through the interposition of a shabby charlatan who took money for the exhibition of his power.

"I sat in the darkness, bored and disgusted, utterly incurious, desiring nothing but the close of the manifestations and escape into the open air, when suddenly, in a faint light, which came I knew not whence, I saw a face on the opposite side of the circle of faces, a face which assuredly had not been among the audience before the lamp was darkened at the beginning of the *séance*. Yet so far as my sense of hearing, which was particularly acute, could inform me, no door had opened, no footstep had crossed the floor since we had seated ourselves at the table, and had formed the circle, hand touching hand.

"This hitherto unseen face had a wan and mournful beauty which at once changed my feelings from apathy to interest. The eyes were of a lovely blue, and were remarkable for that translucent brilliancy which is rarely seen after childhood; the features were delicate to attenuation, and, in the faint light, the cheeks looked hollow and colourless, and even the lips were of a sickly pallor. The loveliness of those large ethereal eyes counterbalanced all want of life and colour in the rest of the face, which, had those eyes been hidden under lowered lids, might have seemed the face of the dead. I looked at it, awe-stricken. Its presence had in one instant transformed the scene of vulgar imposture to a temple and a shrine. I watched and waited, spell-bound.

"There were subdued whisperings round the table, and a general excitement and expectancy which indicated the beginning of a more enthralling performance than the vagabond rappings on table and wainscot, or even the furtive and flying touch of smooth cold hands.

"For some minutes, for an interval that seemed much longer than it really was, nothing happened.

"The face looked at us—or, rather, looked beyond us; the pale lips were parted as in prayer or invocation; the long yellow hair streaming over the shoulders gleamed faintly in the dim, uncertain light, which came and went from some mysterious source. The door opening on the entrance hall was behind my side of the table, and I have little doubt that the curiously soft and searching light, which fluttered every now and then across the circle and lingered on the face opposite, was manipulated by some one outside the door.

"Presently there came a shower of raps—here, there, everywhere, on ceiling, wainscot, doors, above our heads, under our feet—while a strain of organ music, so softly played as to seem remote, crept into the room, and increased the confusion of our senses, distracted past endurance by those meaningless rappings.

"Suddenly a young woman at the end of the table gave a hysterical cry.

"'She is rising, she is rising!' she said. 'Oh, to think of it, to think of it! To think how He rose—He whom they had slain—and vanished from the loving eyes of His disciples! She is like the angels who gather round His throne. Who can doubt now?'

"'It's humbug, and we all know it's humbug,' grumbled the sea-dog on my right. 'But it's clever humbug; and it isn't easy to catch them napping.'

"'Hush!' said the professor's wife indignantly. 'Watch her, and be silent.'

"We watched. I had not once taken my eyes from that pale, spiritual face, with the eyes that had a look of seeing things in an immeasurable distance—the things that are not of this earth. Suddenly the dreamy tranquillity of the countenance changed to violent emotion, an ecstatic smile parted the pale lips, and, for the first time since I had been conscious of her presence, those exquisite lips spoke.

"'It is coming, it is coming!' she cried. 'Take me, take me, take me!' And then from speech to song seemed a natural transition, as she sang in a silver-sweet soprano—

"'Angels ever bright and fair,
Take, oh take me to your care.'

"As that lovely melody floated through the room, the slender, girlish form was wafted slowly upward with steady, gradual motion, until it hovered halfway between the ceiling and the floor, the long white robe flowing far below the feet, the golden hair falling below the waist. Nothing more like the conventional idea of an angelic presence could have offered itself to the excited imagination. The figure remained suspended, the arms lifted, and the semi-transparent hands scattering flowers, while we gazed, enthralled by the beauty and gracefulness of that strange vision, and for the moment the hardest of us, even the sea-dog at my side, was a believer.

"Nothing so beautiful could be false, dishonest, ignoble. No; whatever the rest of the *séance* might be, this at least was no vulgar cheat. We were in the presence of a mysterious being, exceptionally gifted—human, perhaps; but not as the common herd are human.

"I was weak enough to think thus. I had abandoned myself wholly to the glamour of the scene, when the sea-dog started to his feet, as the girl gave a shrill cry of fear. She hung for a moment or two over the table, head downward, and fell in a heap between two of the seated spectators, her head striking against the edge of the table, her long hair streaming wide, and faint moanings as of acute pain issuing from her pallid lips.

"In an instant all was noise and confusion. The sea-captain struck a match, Mr. Ravenshaw produced an end of wax candle, and everybody crowded round the girl, talking and exclaiming unrestrainedly.

"'There, now; didn't I tell you so? All a cheat from beginning to end.'

"'He ought to be prosecuted.'

"'Nobody but fools would have ever believed in such stuff.'

"'Look here!' cried the sea-captain, 'she was held up by a straight iron rod which passes through the floor, and a cross-bar, like a pantomime fairy. She was strapped to the cross-bar, and the strap broke and let her go. She's the artfullest hussy I ever had anything to do with; for I'll be hanged if she hadn't almost taken me in with that face and voice of hers. 'Waft me, angels,' and looking just like an angel, and all the time this swindler was strapping her on to the iron bar.'

"The swindler defended himself angrily, in a jumble of German and English, getting more German as he grew more desperate. They were all clamouring round him. The flaxen-headed Frau had slipped away in the beginning of the skirmish. The golden-haired girl had fainted—a genuine faint, apparently, whatever else might be false—and her head was lying on Mrs. Ravenshaw's shoulder; that lady's womanly compassion for helpless girlhood being stronger even than her indignation at having been hoaxed.

"'Give us back our money!' cried three or four voices out of the dimness. 'Give us back our money for the whole series of *séances*!'

"'Half-guinea tickets! Dear enough if the thing had been genuine!'

"'An impudent swindle!'

"'Will somebody run for the police?' said the sea-captain. 'I'll stay and take care they don't give us the slip. Who'll go?'

"There were half a dozen volunteers, who began to grope their way to the door.

"'One's enough,' said the sea-captain. 'Take care that fellow doesn't make a bolt of it.'

"The warning came too late. As he spoke, spirit-lips blew out the candle which Mr. Ravenshaw was patiently holding above the group of fainting girl and kindly woman, like one of the living candlesticks in the 'Legend of Montrose,' and the room was dark. There was a sound of scuffling, a rush, the door opened and shut again, and a key turned in the lock with decisive emphasis.

"'Done!' cried the sea-captain, making his way to the curtained window.

"It was curtained and shuttered, and the opening of the shutters occupied some minutes, even for the seaman's practised hands. There were bolts—old-fashioned bolts—with mechanism designed to defy burglary, in the days when wealth and fashion inhabited Bloomsbury. Wax matches sputtered and emitted faint gleams and flashes of light here and there in the room. Two or three people had found their way to the locked door, and were shaking and kicking it savagely, without effect.

"At last the bolts gave way, the deft hands having found the trick of them. The seaman flung open the shutters, and the light of the street-lamp streamed into the room.

"The girl was still unconscious, lying across two chairs, her head on the novelist's shoulder.

"'Shamming, no doubt,' said the seaman.

"'No, no; there is no acting here,' said the lady. 'Her face and hands are deadly cold. Ah, she is beginning to recover. How she shudders, poor child!'

"A long-drawn, shivering sob broke from the white lips, which I could see faintly in uncertain light from the street-lamp. The seaman was talking to some one outside, asking him to send the first policeman he met, or to go to the nearest police-office and send some one from there.

"'What's the matter?' asked the voice outside. 'Anybody hurt?'

"'No; but I want to give some one in charge.'

"'All right,' said the voice; and then we heard footsteps hurrying off.

"'Whom are you going to give in charge?' asked Mr. Ravenshaw, in his calm, practical way. 'Not this shivering girl, surely. The other birds are flown.'

"'She may shiver,' retorted the seaman angrily. 'I shall be glad to see her shiver before the beak, to-morrow. He'll talk to her. Shivering won't get over *him*. He's used to it. Of course she's fainted. A woman can always faint when she finds herself in a difficulty. We'll have her up for obtaining money upon false pretences, all the same.'

"The united efforts of three or four of the party had burst open the door of the room, and everybody except the little group about the girl—myself among them—made for the street door, which was not locked.

"A couple of policemen arrived a few minutes afterwards, and thereupon began a severe inspection of the house from cellar to garret. They found an old woman in a back kitchen, who explained that the dining and drawing-room floors, and the front kitchen were let to the table-turning gentleman and his wife, and the young lady who lived with them. They had occupied the rooms nearly three months, had paid some rent, but were considerably in arrear. The landlord, who occupied the second floor, had gone into the country to see a sick daughter. Two young men lodged in the attics—printer's readers—but they were seldom in before eleven.

"In a word, the old woman, who was general drudge and caretaker, was alone in the basement with a plethoric spaniel, too old and obese to bark, and a tabby cat. All the rest of the house was empty of human life.

"The policemen and the late believers in Herr Kaltardern's occult powers explored every corner of the rooms which the Germans and their accomplice had inhabited. The personal belongings of the three were of the slightest, the Kaltarderns' sole possession being a large carpet bag of ancient and obsolete fashion, and a brush and comb. The room occupied by the girl was clean and tidy, and contained a respectable-looking wooden trunk.

"The machinery of the imposture stood confessed in this investigation. The bookcase was a dummy piece of furniture which concealed a door of communication between the front and back rooms. Door of room, and door of bookcase, the front of which opened in one piece, were both so artfully padded with baize as to open and shut noiselessly; and it was by this means that the tricksters had been able to bring their innocent accomplice into the room unobserved, or to go in and out themselves while the sceptical among their audience might be watching the only obvious entrance to the room. In the kitchen below the iron rod and the hole through the ceiling plainly indicated the means by which the girl had been lifted off her feet. The transverse bar was attached to the rod in the room above, by the noiseless hands of the professor.

"All this I heard afterwards from Gerald, who took an active part in the investigation. For myself, while the inquisitive explorers were tramping in and out of the rooms above and below, I remained beside the two good people who were caring for the helpless sharer in the foolish show—accomplice or victim, as the case might be.

"I had found and relighted the lamp, and by its light Mrs. Ravenshaw and I examined the girl's forehead, which had been severely cut in her fall. While we were gently drying the blood which stained her eyelids and cheeks, she opened her eyes and looked at us with a bewildered expression.

"'Oh, how my head aches!' she moaned. 'What was it hurt me like that?'

"'You were hurt in your fall,' I answered. 'Your head struck the edge of the table.'

"'But how could I fall? How could they let me fall?'

"'The strap round your waist broke, and you fell from the iron bar.'

"She looked at me in amazement—simulated, as I thought—and it distressed me to think that fair young face should be capable of such a lying look.

"'What strap? The spirits were holding me up—wafting me towards the sky.'

"'Very likely,' I answered, picking up the broken strap and showing it to her; 'but the spirits couldn't manage it without a little mechanical aid. And the mechanical aid was not as sound as it ought to have been.'

"The girl took the strap in her hands, and looked at it and felt it with an expression of countenance so full of hopeless bewilderment that I began to doubt my previous conviction, to doubt even the evidence of my senses. Could any youthful face be so trained to depict unreal emotion? Could so childlike a creature be such a consummate actress?

"'Was this round my waist?' she asked, looking from me to the kind-hearted woman whose arms were still supporting her slender, undeveloped figure.

"'Yes, this was round your waist, and by this you were strapped to this iron bar here. You see, the rod passes through the floor. The cross-bar must have been fastened to it while you were singing. My poor child, pray do not try to sustain a falsehood. You are so young that you are hardly responsible for what you have done. You were in these people's power, and they could make you do what they liked. Pray be candid with us. We want to befriend you if we can, do we not, Mrs. Ravenshaw?'

"'Yes, indeed we do, poor thing!' answered the lady heartily. 'Only be truthful with us.'

"'Indeed, I am telling the truth,' the girl protested tearfully. 'I did not know of that strap, or of the iron rod. They told me I was gifted—that I was in communion with my dear dead father, when I felt my soul uplifted—as I have felt it often and often, sitting singing to myself, alone in my room. I have felt as if my spirit were soaring away and away, upward to that world beyond the skies where my father and my mother are. I have felt as if, while my body remained below, my spirit were floating upward and upward, away from earth and sorrow. I told the Frau how I used to feel, because I believed in her. She brought me into communion with my father. He used to rap out messages of love; and she taught me how to understand the spirit language. That was how I came to know her. That was how I was willing to go with them and join in their *séances*.'

"'I begin to understand,' said I. 'They told you that you were gifted, and that you had a power of floating upward from the floor to the ceiling?'

"'Yes. It came upon me unawares. They asked me to sing, and to let my spirit float towards heaven as I sang. I always used to feel like that of an evening in our church in the country. I used to feel my soul lifted upward when I sang the *Magnificat*. And one night at a *séance*, soon after we came to London, I was singing, and I felt myself floating upward. It seemed as if some powerful hands were holding me up; and I felt round me in the half-darkness, and there was no one near. I was moving alone, without any visible help; and I felt that it was the passionate longing of my spirit to approach the spirit of my dead father which was lifting me up. And, oh, was it only that horrid strap and that iron rod?' she exclaimed, bursting into tears. 'How cruel—how cruel to cheat me like that!'

"She had evidently no thought of the public who were cheated, or of her own position as a detected impostor, or the tool and accomplice of impostors. Her tears were for the dream so rudely broken.

"The tramping in and out of rooms was over by this time. The majority of the audience were leaving the house, the sea-dog loud in his disgust and indignation till the last moment.

"'I should have liked to give that young hussey in charge,' he said in a loud voice as he passed the half-open door, evidently arguing with some milder-tempered victim; 'but, as you say, she's little more than a child, and no magistrate would punish her.'

"I breathed more freely when I heard the street door bang behind this gentleman and the policemen.

"'They're all gone except ourselves,' said Gerald. 'The gifted German and his wife have shown us a clean pair of heels, and there's only an old charwoman in the basement. She tells me your young friend there came from the country—somewhere in Sussex—and always behaved herself very nicely. The old woman seems fond of her.'

"'Yes, she was always kind to me,' said the girl.

"'Was she? Well, I hope she'll be kind to you now you're left high and dry,' said Gerald. 'These people won't come back any more, I take it. They travel in light marching order—a grubby old carpet bag, and a brush and comb which would account for the lady's tangled head. They won't come back to fetch *those*, at the risk of being had up for obtaining money upon false pretences. And what's to become of you, I wonder?'—to the girl. 'Have you any money?'

"'No, sir.'

"'Any friends in London?'

"'No.'

"'Any friends in the country—in the place you left?'

"'Not now. No one would be kind to me now. There was a kind lady who wanted to apprentice me to her dressmaker when my father died, and I was left quite alone; but I hated the idea of dressmaking; and one night there was a spiritualistic *séance* at the school-house, and I went, because I had heard of messages from the dead, and I thought if it were possible for the dead to speak to the living, my father would not leave me without one word of consolation. We loved each other so dearly; we were all the world to each other; and people said the dead had spoken—had sent messages of love and comfort. So I went to the dark *séance*, and I asked them to call my father's spirit; and there was a message rapped out, and I believed that it was from him; and next day I met Madame Kaltardern in the street, and I asked her if the messages were really true; and she said they were true, and she spoke very kindly to me, and asked me if I would like to be a medium, and said she was sure I was gifted—I could be a clairvoyant if I liked—she could see from the shape of my eyes that I had the power, and it would be a great pity for me not to use it. She said it was a glorious life to be in constant communion with great spirits.'

"'And you thought you would like it better than dressmaking?' said Mrs. Ravenshaw, sympathetically.

"'It was of my father I thought. He had been dead such a short time. Sometimes I could hardly believe that he was dead. When I sat alone in the firelight, I used to fancy he was in the room with me; I used to speak to him, and beg him to answer me.'

"'And were there any raps then?' asked the practical Ravenshaw.

"'No, never when I was alone. The Kaltarderns came back after Christmas, and there was another *séance*, for the benefit of the Infirmary, and I went again; and Madame told me my father was speaking to me. He rapped out a strange message about the organ. I was to bid good-bye to the organ of which I was so fond; for I had a gift that was greater than music; and I was to go with those who could cultivate that gift. So the next day, when Madame Kaltardern asked me to go away with them, and promised to develop my mediumistic power, I consented to go. I was to be like their adopted daughter. They were to clothe me and feed me, but they were to give me no money. A gift like mine could not be paid for with money. If I tried to make money by my power, I should lose it. I did not want money from them. I wanted to be brought into communion with the spirit world, with my father whom I loved so dearly, and with my mother, who died when I was eight years old, and with my little sister Lucy, who died soon after mother—the little sister I used to nurse. My only world was the world of the dead. And, oh, was it all trickery—all? Those messages from father and mother—those baby kisses, so soft, so quick, so light; the hand upon my forehead—the hand of the dead—touching me and blessing me! Was it all false, all trickery?'

"She rocked herself to and fro sobbing, unconsolable at the thought of her vanished dream-world.

"'I'm afraid so, my dear,' said Ravenshaw, kindly. 'I'm afraid it was all humbug. You have been duped yourself, while you have helped to dupe others. It was uncommonly clever of them to get an unconscious accomplice. And now what is to be done with this poor thing? That is the question,' he concluded, appealing to his wife and me.

"'Yes, that's the question with a vengeance,' said Gerald. 'We can't leave her in this house in the care of a deaf old woman, to bear the brunt of the landlord's anger when he comes home and finds the birds flown and his arrears of rent the baddest of bad debts. Poor child! we must get her away somehow. Have you no friends in the country who would give you a home?' he asked the girl.

"'No,' she answered, fighting with her sobs. 'People were very kind to me just at first after my father's death; and then I think they got tired of me. They said I was helpless; I ought to have been able to put my hand to something useful. The only thing I cared for was music. I used to sing in the choir; but it was only a village church, and the choir were only paid a pound a quarter. I couldn't live upon that; and I couldn't play the organ well enough to take my father's place. And then Miss Grimshawe, a rich old lady, offered to apprentice me to a dressmaker; but I hated the idea of that. Dressmakers' girls are so common; and my father was a gentleman, though he was poor. When I told Miss Grimshawe I was going away with the Kaltarderns, she was very angry. She said I should end badly. Everybody was angry. I can never go back to them; they would all turn from me.'

"Mr. Ravenshaw looked suspicious; Mrs. Ravenshaw looked serious; and even I asked myself whether the girl's story, so plausible, so convincing to my awakened interest, might not, after all, be a tissue of romance, which sounded natural, because it had been recited so often.

"Gerald was the most business-like among us.

"'What is your name?' he asked.

"'Esperanza Campbell.'

"'Esperanza? Why, that's a Spanish name!'

"'My mother was a Spaniard.'

"'So! And what is the name of the village where your father played the organ?'

"'Besbery, near Petworth.'

"'Besbery!' repeated Gerald, pencilling memoranda on his linen cuff. 'Do you remember the name of the vicar, or rector?'

"'There was only a curate-in-charge—Mr. Harrison.'

"'Very good,' said Gerald.' Now, what we have to do is to get this poor young lady into a decent lodging, where the landlady will take care of her till we can help her to find some employment, or respectable situation, not mediumistic. I suppose it would hardly be convenient to you to take her home with you, and keep her for a week or so, Mrs. Ravenshaw?' Gerald inquired, as an afterthought.

"Mrs. Ravenshaw hastened to explain that, with children, nursery-governess, and spinster aunt, every bed in her house at Shooter's Hill was occupied.

"'We have not known what it is to have a spare bedroom for the last three years,' she said.

"'Babies have accumulated rather rapidly,' said Ravenshaw. Poor creature, how my careless, independent bachelorhood pitied him! 'And every second baby means another servant. If one could only bring them up in a frame, like geranium cuttings!'

"'I think I know of a lodging-house where Miss Campbell could find a temporary home, not far from here,' I said.

"'Think you know?' cried Gerald, impatiently. 'You can't think about knowing; you know or don't know. Where is it?'

"'In Great Ormond Street.'

"'Capital—close by. I'll go and get a cab. Miss Campbell, just put your traps together, and—and do up your hair, and get on a gown,' looking at her flowing robe and dishevelled hair with evident distaste, 'while I'm gone.'

"He was out of the room in a moment.

"'Are you sure the house is perfectly respectable, Mr. Beresford?' inquired Mrs. Ravenshaw, who, as a fiction-weaver, no doubt let her imagination run upon the horrors of the great city and the secret iniquities of lodging-house keepers, from Hogarth's time downwards.

"I told her that I could trust my own sister to the house in Great Ormond Street, which was kept by my old nurse and my father's old butler, who had retired from service about five years before, and had invested their savings in the furnishing of a spacious old-fashioned house in a district where rents were then low, for the accommodation of all that is most respectable in the way of families and single gentlemen.

"'I can vouch for my old nurse Martha as one of the best and kindest of women, as well as one of the shrewdest,' I said.

"The girl heard this discussion unmoved and uninterested by the trouble we were taking on her behalf. Her sobs had subsided, but she was crying silently, weeping over the cruel end of a dream which had been more to her than all the waking world. She told me afterwards how much and how real that dream had been to her.

"Mrs. Ravenshaw went to her room with her, and helped her to exchange the long white alb-like garment for a tidy black gown, on which the crape trimming had grown rusty with much wear. I can see her now as she came back into the lamplight in that plain black gown, and with her yellow hair rolled into a massive coil at the back of her head, the graceful figure, so girlish, so willowy in its tall slenderness, the fair pale face, and dark-blue eyes heavy with tears.

"She had a poor little black-straw hat in her hand, which she put on presently, before we went downstairs to the cab. Gerald and I carried her box. There was no one to object to its removal. The old woman in the basement made no sign. One of the printers let himself in with a latch-key while we were in the hall, looked at us curiously, and went upstairs without a word.

"Mrs. Ravenshaw kissed Esperanza, and wished her a friendly good night, promising to do what she could to help her in the future; and then she and her husband hurried away to catch the last train to Shooter's Hill."

CHAPTER VIII
"WHAT WAS A SPECK EXPANDS INTO A STAR"

"Had the landlady of the house in Great Ormond Street been anybody in the world except my old nurse, I doubt if any philanthropic purpose would have inspired me with the boldness to carry through the work I had undertaken. To appear before the average lodging-house keeper within half an hour of midnight, and with such a *protégée* as Esperanza Campbell upon my hands, would have required the courage of a lion; and I was at that time a particularly shy and sensitive young man, brought up in the retirement of a country house and in the society of a mother whom I loved very dearly, but, as we are told to love God, with fear and trembling. My constitutional shyness, the natural outcome of narrow surroundings, had kept me from making friends at the University, and I believe it was sheer pity that had prompted Gerald Standish to take me under his wing. His kindness was rewarded by finding me a likable companion, whose character supplied some of the qualities which were wanting in his bright and buoyant disposition. We were real friends; and remained friends until the end of his too-brief life.

"So much to explain that it was only my confidence in my old nurse's indulgence which enabled me to cut the knot of the difficulty in disposing of Esperanza Campbell.

"My faithful Martha and her excellent husband were sleeping the sleep of the just in a ground-floor room at the back of the house, while their maid-servant slumbered still more soundly in a back attic. Happily Martha was a light sleeper, had trained herself to wake at the lightest cry in seasons of measles or whooping-cough, teething or infantile bronchitis; so my second application to the bell and knocker brought a prompt response. Bolts were drawn, a key was turned, a chain was unfastened, the door was opened a couple of inches, and a timid voice asked what was wanted.

"'It is I, Martha, George Beresford. I've brought you a lodger.'

"'Oh, come now, Mr. George, that's one of your jokes. You've been to the theatre, and you're playing a trick upon me. Go home now, do, like a dear young gentleman, and come and have a cup of tea with me some afternoon when you've got half an hour to spare.'

"'Martha, you are keeping a very sweet young lady out in the cold. For goodness' sake, open the door, and let me explain matters.'

"'Can't she take her in?' asked Gerald, impatiently, from the cab.

"Martha opened the door, and exhibited herself reluctantly in her casual costume of flannel dressing-gown and tartan shawl.

"'What *do* you mean, Mr. George? What can you mean by wanting lodgings for a young lady at this time of night?'

"'Sounds queer, don't it?' said Gerald, who had bounded up the steps and burst into the wainscoted hall, lighted only by the candle Martha was carrying. 'The fact is, we're in a difficulty, and Mr. Beresford assures me you can get us out of it.'

"And then in fewest words and with most persuasive manner he explained what we wanted, a home and a protector for a blameless young girl whom the force of circumstances had flung upon our hands at half-past eleven o'clock in the evening. Somehow we must get rid of her. She was a gentleman's daughter, and we could not take her to the workhouse. Reputation, hers and ours, forbade that we should take her to an hotel.

"Not a word did Gerald say about table-turning or spirit-rapping. He was shrewd enough to guess that any hint at the *séance* would have prejudiced honest Martha against our charge.

"'I'm sure I don't know what to do,' said Martha; and I could see that she was suspicious of Gerald's airy manner, and doubtful even of me. 'My husband's fast asleep. He isn't such a light sleeper as I am. I don't know what he would say——'

"'Never mind what he would say,' interrupted Gerald. 'What you have to say is that you'll take Miss Campbell in and give her a tidy room somewhere—she ain't particular, poor thing!—and make her comfortable for a week or two while she looks out for a situation.'

"'Oh, she's on the look-out for a situation, is she?' said Martha, evidently mollified by the idea of a bread-winning young person. 'You see, Mr. George,' she went on, appealing to me, 'in London one can't be too particular. This house is what Benjamin and I have to look to in our old age; we've put our little all into it; and if the young lady happened to be rather dressy; or sang comic songs; or went to the theatre in cabs; or had gentlemen leave letters for her; why, it would just be our ruin. Our first floor is let to one of the most particular of widow ladies. I don't believe there's a more particular lady in London.'

"'My dear Martha, do you think I'm a fool or a knave? This girl is a village organist's daughter— —'

"'Ah, Mr. George, they must all begin,' said Martha, shaking her head philosophically.

"'She is in mourning for her father—an orphan—friendless and unhappy— —'

"'As for conduct, propriety, and all that kind of thing, I'll answer for her as if she were my own sister,' put in Gerald, in his splendidly reckless way; 'and that being the case, I hope you are not going to keep the poor young lady sitting out there in a cold cab till to-morrow morning.'

"Martha listened to Gerald, and looked at me.

"'If you're sure it's all right, Mr. George,' she murmured, 'I'd do anything in the world to oblige you; but this house is our all— —'

"'Yes, yes,' Gerald exclaimed impatiently. 'You told us that before. Bring her in, George. It's all settled.'

"This was a happy stroke, for old Martha would have stood in the hall with her guttering candle and in her deshabille of flannel and tartan debating the matter for another quarter of an hour; but when I brought the pale girl in her black frock up the steps, and handed her into the old woman's care, the motherly heart melted in a moment, and hesitancy was at an end.

"'Poor young thing; why, she's little more than a child! How pale and cold you look, poor dear. I'll go down and light a bit of fire and warm a cup of broth for you. My second floor left the day before yesterday. I'll soon get the bedroom ready for you.'

"'That's as it should be,' said I. 'You'll find yourself safe and comfortable here, Miss Campbell, with the kindest woman I know. I'll call in a few days, and see how you are getting on.'

"I slipped a couple of sovereigns into my old nurse's palm as I wished her good night. The cabman brought in the poor little wooden trunk, received a liberal fare, and went his way in peace, while Gerald and I walked to the Tavistock, glad to cool down after the evening's excitement.

"'What an adventure!' said he. 'Of course I always knew it was humbug, but I never thought it was quite such transparent humbug.'

"'That girl would have taken any one in,' said I.

"'What, because she's young and pretty, after a rather sickly fashion?'

"'No, because she was so thoroughly in earnest, and believed in the thing herself.'

"'You really think she was a dupe and not an accomplice?'

"'I am sure of it. Her distress was unmistakable. And at her age, and with her imaginative nature— —'

"'What did you know of her nature?' he asked sharply.

"The question and his manner of asking it pulled me up suddenly, as a dreamer of morning dreams is awakened by the matter-of-fact voice of the servant who comes to call him.

"What did I know of her? What assurance had I that her sobs and lamentation, her pathetic story of the father so loved and mourned, were not as spurious as the rest of the show, as much a cheat as the iron rod and the leather strap? How did I know? Well, I could hardly have explained the basis of my conviction, but I did know; and I would have staked my life upon her honesty and her innocence.

"I woke next morning to a new sense of responsibility. I had taken this helpless girl's fate into my hands, and to me she must look for aid in chalking out a path for herself. I had to find her the means of earning her daily bread, reputably, and not as a drudge. The problem was difficult of solution. I had heard appalling descriptions of the lot of the average half-educated governess—the life harder, the pay less, than a servant's. Yet what better than a nursery governess could this girl be? at her age, and with her attainments, which I concluded were not above the ordinary schoolgirl's. The look-out was gloomy, and I was glad to shut my eyes to the difficulties of the situation, telling myself that my good Martha would give the poor child a comfortable home upon very moderate terms—such terms as I could afford to pay out of my very moderate allowance, and that in a month or two something—in the language of the immortal Micawber—would turn up.

"There was but another week of the Long, a week which under ordinary conditions I should have spent with my widowed mother at her house in the country, but which I decided to spend in London, accepting Gerald's invitation to share his rooms in Arundel Street, and do a final round of the theatres; an invitation I had previously declined. During that week I was often in Great Ormond Street, and contrived to learn a great deal more about Esperanza's character and history. Of her history all she had to tell;

of her character, which to me seemed transparent as a forest streamlet, all I could divine. I called in Ormond Street on the second day of her residence there, and found good Nurse Martha in the best possible humour. It was four o'clock in the afternoon, and she insisted that I should stop for a cup of tea, and as tea-making—that is to say, the art of producing a better cup of tea than anybody else could produce from the same cannister, kettle, and teapot—had always been a special talent of Martha's, I was glad to accept her hospitality.

"Miss Campbell had gone for a little walk round the squares, she informed me.

"'She doesn't care about going out,' explained Martha; 'she'd rather sit over a book or play the harmonium. But I told her she must take an airing for her health's sake.'

"I was disappointed at not finding Esperanza in the tidy back parlour to which Nurse Martha ushered me—a room of exemplary neatness and snugness, enlivened by those living presences which always make for cheerfulness—vulgar as we may deem them—a glass tank of gold fish, a canary bird, and a magnificent tabby cat, sleek, clean, luxuriously idle, in purring contemplation of the bright little fire in the old-fashioned grate, that grate with hobs which reminded me of my nursery deep in the heart of the country.

"'Now you sit down in Blake's armchair, Mr. George, and let's have a talk over missy. I shouldn't have taken those two sovereigns from you the night before last if I hadn't been all of a muddle with the suddenness of the thing. I don't want to be paid in advance for doing a kindness to a helpless girl.'

"'No, Martha; but since the helpless girl was on my hands, it's only right I should pay you somehow, and we may as well settle that question at once, as it may be several weeks before Miss Campbell is able to find a suitable situation.'

"'Several months, more likely. Do you know how young she is, Mr. George?'

"'Eighteen.'

"'Eighteen last birthday—only just turned eighteen, and she's much younger than most girls of eighteen in all her ways and thoughts. She's clever enough with her hands, poor child. Nothing lazy or lolloping about her—made her own bed and swept and tidied her own room without a word from me; but there's a helplessness somewhere. I believe the weakness is in her thoughts. I don't know how she'll ever set about getting a situation—I don't know what kind of situation she's fit for. She's much too young and too pretty for a governess.'

"'Not too young for a nursery-governess, surely.'

"'A nursery-governess means a nursery-maid without a cap, Mr. George. I shouldn't like to see her brought to that. I've taken to her already. Benjamin says, with her sweet voice and pretty face, she ought to go on the stage.'

"I was horrified at the idea.

"'Martha, how can you speak of such a thing? Have you any idea of what the life of a theatre means for an inexperienced girl—for a beautiful girl, most of all?'

"'Oh, I've heard there are temptations; but a prudent young woman can take care of herself anywhere, Mr. George; and an imprudent young woman will go wrong in a country parsonage, or in a nunnery. If Miss Campbell is to earn her own living, she'll have to face dangers and temptations, go where she may. She'll have to take care of herself, poor child. There'll be nobody else to take care of her. I've heard that young women are well looked after in the better class of theatres—at Mr. Charles Kean's, for instance. I knew a young person that used to walk on in *Louis the Eleventh*—dressed as a page, in blue and gold—and she told me that Mr. and Mrs. Charles Kean was *that* particular——'

"'The Keans are making a farewell tour in Australia, and will never go into management again, Martha. You are talking nonsense.'

"Poor Martha looked crestfallen at this reproof.

"'I dare say I am, Mr. George; but, for all that, I don't think Miss Campbell will ever do much as a governess. It isn't in her. There's a helplessness, and a bendingness, and droopingness, if I may say so, about her character that won't do for a governess. The only mistress that would keep her is the kind of mistress that would make a slave of her.'

"'Hard lines,' I said, getting up and walking about the little back parlour.

"It was a third room quite at the back of the substantial Georgian house; and there was scant space for my restlessness between the old square piano, which served as a sideboard, and the fireplace by which my dear old Martha sat looking at me with a perturbed countenance.

"I began to think I had let myself in for a bad thing. What was I to do with this girl, whose fate I had in some measure taken into my hands? It had seemed easy enough to bring her to this quiet shelter, which she might leave in a week or so, braced up and ready to fight her battle of life—the battle we all have to fight somehow—a self-supporting young woman. Self-supporting, that was the point. I now remembered with terror that there is a large class of persons upon this earth whom not even the scourge of poverty can make self-supporting; a vast multitude of feeble souls who resign themselves from the beginning of things to drift upon the stream of life, and are never known to strike out and swim for any shore, and so drift down to the ocean of death. Of these are the poor relations for whom something is for ever being done, and who never do anything for themselves; of these the feeble scions of patrician family trees, who are always waiting for sinecures under Government.

"God help her, poor soul, if she was one of these invertebrates; and God help me in my responsibility towards her.

"I was an only son; the heir to a small estate in Suffolk, and an income of something under three thousand a year. I was not quite twenty years of age, and I had to maintain myself at the most expensive college in Cambridge on an allowance that many of the rich young men with whom I associated would have considered abject penury. I was not in a fast set. I did not hunt—indeed, with my modest income, hunting would have been impossible; but I was not without tastes which absorbed money; the love of choice books and fine engravings, the fancy for curios picked up here or there, the presence of which gave interest to my rooms, and, perhaps, helped to reconcile me to many long hours within closed doors. I had hitherto been most careful to live within my income, for I knew that it was as much as my mother could afford to give me, taking into consideration her devotion to the estate which was to be mine by-and-by, and the maintenance and improvement of which had been to her as a religion. Her model cottages, her home-farm, the village church, to whose every improvement her purse had largely contributed, these were the sources of expenditure which kept her comparatively poor, and which forbade any kind of extravagance on my part.

"All these facts were in my mind that afternoon as I paced the narrow bounds of old Martha's sitting-room.

"'She will have to get her living,' I said severely, as the result of these meditations, which showed me no surplus income for philanthropy.

"Had my mother been as some men's mothers, I might naturally have contemplated shifting the burden upon her shoulders. I might have told her Esperanza's story, and handed Esperanza over to her care as freely as if I had picked up a stray cat or dog. But my mother was not one of those soft, impressionable women who are always ready to give the reins to sentiment. She was a good woman, and devoted much of her life and means to doing good, but her benevolence was restricted to the limits of her parish. She would hardly listen to a tale of sorrow outside her own village.

"'We have so much to do for our own people, George,' she used to tell me; 'it is folly to be distracted by outside claims. Here we know our return for every shilling we give. We know the best and the worst about those we help.'

"Were I to tell her Esperanza's story, her suggestions for helping me out of my difficulty would be crueller than old Martha's. She would be for sending the girl into service as a housemaid, or for getting her an assisted passage to the Antipodes on an emigrant ship.

"Martha came to my rescue in my trouble now as she had done many a time when I wore a kilt, and when my naked knees had come into abrupt collision with a gravel path or a stony beach.

"'She'll have to be older and wiser before she gets her own living, Mr. George,' said Martha; 'but don't you trouble about her. As long as I've a bed or a sofa to spare, she can stop with me and Benjamin. Her bite and sup won't hurt us, poor thing, and I don't want sixpence from you. She shall stop here free gratis, Mr. George, till she finds a better home.'

"I gave my old nurse a hug, as if I had been still the boy in the Macdougal kilt.

"'No, no, Martha; I'm not going to impose on your generosity. I shall be able to pay you *something*. Only I thought you might want two or three pounds a week for her board, and I could not manage that for an indefinite period."

"'Two or three pounds! Lor, Mr. George, if that's your notion of prices, Cambridge land-ladies must be 'arpies. Why, I only get two guineas for my drawing-room floor, as a permanency, and lady-tenants even begrudge half a crown extra for kitchen fire. Let her stop here as long as she likes, Mr. George, and never you think about money. It's only her future I'm thinking of, for there's a helplessness about her that— —Ah, there she is,' as the hall door slowly opened. 'I gave her my key. She's quite one of us already.'

"She came quietly into the room, and took my offered hand without shyness or embarrassment. She was pale still, but the fresh air had brought a faint tint of rose into the wan cheeks. She looked even younger and more childlike to-day in her shabby mourning frock and poor little black straw hat than she had looked the night before last. Her strong emotion then had given more of womanliness to the small oval face. To-day there was a simplicity in her aspect, as of a trusting child who took no thought of the future, secure in the kindness of those about her.

"I thought of a sentence in the gospel. 'Consider the lilies how they grow.' This child had grown up like a lily in the mild atmosphere of domestic love, and had been the easy dupe of a delusion which appealed to her affection for the dead.

"'I called to see if you were quite comfortable and at home with Mrs. Blake,' I said, far more embarrassed by the situation than Esperanza was.

"'Yes, indeed I am,' she answered in her sad sweet voice. 'It is so nice to be with some one so kind and clean and comfortable. The Frau was not *very* unkind; but she was so dirty. She gave us such horrid things to eat—the smell of them made me ill—and then she said I was affected and silly, and the Herr used to say I might starve if I could not eat their food. It made me think of my happy home with father, and our cosy little tea-table beside the fire. We did not always have dinner,' she added naively; 'neither of us cared much for that.'

"She hung over old Martha's shoulder with affectionate familiarity, and the horny old hand which had led my infant steps was held up to clasp hers, and the withered old face smiled.

"'See how she gets round us,' said Martha, nodding at me. 'Benjamin is just as bad. And you should hear her play the 'armonian of an evening, and sing 'Abide with me.' You'd hardly hear her without shedding tears.'

"'Do you think you can be happy here for a few weeks?' I asked.

"'Yes, as happy as I can be anywhere without father. I dreamt of him last night—such a vivid dream. I know he was near me. It was something more than a dream. I heard his voice close beside my pillow calling my name. I know his spirit was in the room. It isn't because the Herr and his wife were cheats that there is *no* link between the living and the dead. I know there is a link,' she insisted passionately, her eyes brimming with sudden tears. 'They are not dead—those we dearly love—only removed from us. The clay is gone; the soul is hovering near, blessing, comforting us.'

"She sobbed out her grief, hiding her face upon Martha's substantial shoulder. I could speak no word of consolation; nor would I for worlds have argued against this fond hallucination, the dream of sorrowing love.

"'I shall not see thee. Dare I say
No spirit ever brake the band
That stays him from the native land,
Where first he walk'd when clasp't in clay?

No visual shade of some one lost,
But he, the Spirit himself, may come
Where all the nerve of sense is numb;
Spirit to Spirit, Ghost to Ghost.'

"I quoted those lovely lines in a low voice as I walked softly up and down the darkening room; and then there was silence save for soothing wordless murmurs from Martha, such murmurs as had served to hush my own baby sorrows.

"'There's the kettle just on the boil,' cried the great soul, cheerily, when Esperanza's sobs had ceased; 'and I know Mr. George must be wanting his cup of tea.'

"She rose and bustled about in her dear old active way. She lit a lamp—an inartistic cheap paraffin-lamp, but the light was cheerful. The tea-table arranged by Martha was the picture of neatness. She set Esperanza the feminine task of making toast. The poor child had the prettiest air of penitence as she kissed Martha's hand, and then knelt meekly down, with the fireglow crimsoning the alabaster face and neck, and shining on the pale gold hair and rusty black frock.

"'I'm afraid I'm very troublesome,' she said apologetically; 'but, indeed, I'm very grateful to you, sir, for taking care of me that dreadful night, and to dear Mrs. Blake for all her kindness to me.'

"'Mrs. Blake is the quintessence of kindness. I am very glad to think you can live happily here until she or I can find some nice situation for you.'

"She had been smiling softly over her task, but her face clouded in an instant.

"'A situation. That's what everybody said at Besbery! We must find her a situation. And then Miss Grimshaw wanted me to be a dressmaker.'

"'You shall not be a dressmaker. I promise that.'

"'But, oh, what am I to be? I don't know half enough for a governess. I couldn't teach big girls German and French and drawing. I couldn't teach little boys Latin. And that's what everybody wants of a governess. I've read the advertisements in the newspapers.'

"'And as to being a nursery-governess, why, it's negro slavery!' said Martha.

"'I wouldn't mind the drudgery, only I hate children!" said Esperanza.

"This avowal shocked me. I looked at the soft, childlike countenance, and the speech seemed incongruous.

"'I have never had anything to do with children since my sister Lucy died,' she explained. 'I shouldn't understand them, and they would laugh at me and my fancies. After Lucy's death, I lived alone with father, always alone, he and I. The harmonium and the organ in the church close by were our only friends. Our clergyman was just civil to father, but I don't think he ever liked him. I heard him once tell the Bishop that his organist was an eccentricity. An eccentricity! That was all he could say about my father, who was ever so much cleverer than he.'

"She said this with pride, almost with defiance, looking me in the face as if she were challenging me to dispute the fact.

"'Was your father very clever?' I asked her, keenly interested in any glimpses of her history.

"'Yes, I am sure he was clever, much cleverer than the common run of people. He loved music, and he played beautifully. His touch upon the old organ made the church music sound angelic. Now and then there was some one in the church—some stranger—who seemed to understand his playing, and who was astonished to find such an organist in a village church—an out-of-the-way village like ours. But for the most part people took no notice. It didn't seem to matter to them whether the choir sang well or badly; but when they sang false it hurt father just like bodily pain.'

"'Did he teach you to play?'

"'A little. But he wasn't fond of teaching. What I know of music I found out chiefly for myself—just sitting alone at the organ, when I could get one of the choir boys to blow for me, touching the keys, and trying the stops, till I learnt something about them. But I play very badly.'

"'Beautifully! beautifully!' ejaculated Martha. 'You draw tears.'

"'You sang in the choir, I think?' I said.

"'Yes; there were four young ladies, and a lady's-maid with a contralto voice, and I was the sixth. There were about a dozen men and boys, who sat on the other side of the chancel. People said it was a good choir for a village church. Father was so unhappy when we sang badly that we could not help trying hard to sing well.'

"I remembered those seraphic soprano notes in Handel's thrilling melody, and I could understand that at least one voice in the choir had the heavenly ring.

"'Well,' I said at last, 'we must hope for the best. Something may turn up that will suit you better than governessing. And in the mean time you can make yourself happy with my old nurse. I can answer for it she'll never be unkind to you.'

"'I'm sure of that. I would rather stay here and be her servant than go among strangers.'

"'What, wear an apron and cap and wait upon the lodgers?' I said, laughing at the absurdity of the idea. She seemed a creature so far removed from the useful race of neat-handed Phyllises.

"'I should not mind.'

"The clock in the hall struck six, and I had promised Gerald to be ready for dinner at half-past, as we were to go to a theatre afterwards—the Adelphi, where Jefferson was acting in *Rip Van Winkle*. I had to take a hurried leave.

"'Don't you worry yourself about *her*, Mr. George,' said Martha, as she let me out at the street door; ' I'll keep her as long as ever you like.'

"I told Martha that I should send her a little money from time to time, and that I should consider myself in her debt for a pound a week as long as Miss Campbell stayed with her.

"'She'll want a new frock, won't she?' I asked. 'The one she wears looks very shabby.'

"'It looks what it is, Mr. George. It's all but threadbare, and it's the only frock she has in the world, poor child! But don't you trouble about that either. You gave me two sovereigns. One of those will buy the stuff, and she and I can make the frock. I've cut out plenty of frocks in my day. I used to make all your mother's frocks once upon a time.'

"In the bloom of her youth she had nursed my mother; she had nursed me in her sturdy middle life; and now in her old age she was ready and willing to care for this girl for whose fate I had made myself responsible.

"Gerald received me with his customary cheeriness, though I was ten minutes after the half-hour, and the fried sole had frizzled itself to dryness by that delay.

"'I've some good news for you!' he exclaimed, in his exuberant way. 'It's all right.'

"'What's all right?'

"'Your *protégée*. I've written to the parson at Besbery. The story she told us was gospel truth.'

"'I never thought it was anything else.'

"'Ah, that's because you're over head and ears in love with her,' said Gerald.

"I felt myself blushing furiously, blushing like a girl whose secret penchant for the hero of her dreams stands revealed. Of course I protested that nothing was farther from my thoughts than love; that I was only sorry for the girl's loneliness and helplessness. Gerald obviously doubted me; and I had to listen to his sage counsel on the subject. He was my senior by two years, and claimed to be a man of the world, while I had been brought up at my mother's apron-string. He foresaw dangers of which I had no apprehension.

"'There is nothing easier to drop into than an entanglement of that sort,' he said. 'You had much better fall in love with a ballet-girl. It may be more expensive for the moment, and there may be a bigger rumpus about it, but it won't compromise your future.'

"This friendly remonstrance had no effect upon my conduct during the few remaining days of the long vacation. I went to Ormond Street a second and a third time in the course of those few days. I took Esperanza to an afternoon concert at the St. James's Hall, and enjoyed her ecstasy as she listened to Sainton and Bottesini. For her, music was a passion, and I believe she sat beside me utterly unconscious of my existence, with a soul lifted above earth and all earthly feelings.

"'You were happy while the music lasted,' I said, as we walked back to Ormond Street, by a longish round, for I chose the quietest streets rather than the nearest way.

"'More than happy,' she answered softly. 'I was talking with my father's spirit.'

"'You still believe in the communion of the dead and the living,' I said, 'in spite of the tricks your German friends played upon you?'

"'Yes,' she answered steadfastly, 'I still believe. I shall always believe there is a bridge between earth and heaven—between the world we can see and touch and the world we can only feel with our hearts and minds. When I hear music like that we heard just now—those long-drawn singing notes on the violin, those deep organ tones of the 'cello—I feel myself carried away to a shadowy world where I know my father and mother are waiting for me. We shall all be together again some day, and I shall know and understand, and I shall feel her light touch upon my forehead and my hair as I have felt it so often in my dreams.'

"She broke down, crying softly as she walked by my side. I soothed her as well as I could, soothed her most when I talked of those she had lost, questioning her about them. She remembered her mother dimly—a long, last illness, a pale and wasted face, and gentle hands and loving arms that used to be folded round her neck as she nestled against the sick-bed. That sick-room, and the dim light of wintry afternoons, and the sound of the harmonium as her father played soft music in an adjoining parlour, were things that seemed to have lasted for years. She could not look behind them. Her memory of mother and of home stopped on the threshold of that dimly lighted room.

"Her father was a memory of yesterday. He had been her second self, the other half of her mind.

"'He believed in ghosts,' she said, 'and in second sight. He has often told me how he saw my mother coming downstairs to meet him, with a shroud showing faintly above her white summer gown, the night before she broke a blood-vessel and took to her bed in her last illness.'

"'An optical delusion, no doubt; but it comes natural to a Scotchman to believe such things. He should not have told you.'

"'Why not? I like to know that the world we cannot see is near us. I should have died of loneliness if I had not believed my father's spirit was still within reach. I don't mind about those people being impostors. I begin to think that the friends we have lost would hardly talk to us through the moving up and down of wooden tables. It seems such a foolish way, does it not?'

"'Worse than foolish; undignified. The ghosts in Virgil move and talk with a stately grandeur; Shakespeare's ghosts are kingly and awful. They strike terror. It has remained for the nineteenth century to imagine ghosts that flit about a shabby parlour and skip from side to side of the room and flutter round a table, and touch, and rap, and tap, and pat with viscous hands, like the touch of a toad. Samuel Johnson would not have sat up a whole night to see a table heaved up and down, or to be touched on the forehead by a chilly, unknown hand.'

"'I don't care what you say about those things,' she answered resolutely. 'There is a link between life and death. I don't know what the link is; but though my father may be dead to all the world besides he is not dead to me.'

"I did not oppose stubborn common sense to this fond delusion. It might be good for her to believe in the things that are not. The tender fancy might bridge over the dark gulf of sorrow. I tried to divert her mind to lighter subjects—talked to her of this monstrous London of which she knew nothing, and of which I knew very little.

"On the following evening I took Esperanza and my old nurse to a theatre, a form of entertainment in which Martha especially delighted. I was not very happy in my choice of a play. Had I taken my *protégée* to see Jefferson, she would have been touched and delighted. Unluckily I chose another theatre where a burlesque was being played which was just a shade more vulgar than the average burlesque of those days. Esperanza was puzzled and disgusted. I discovered that her love of music was an exclusive passion. She cared for nothing else in the way of art. I tried her with a picture-gallery, only to find her ignorant and indifferent. Two things only impressed her in the whole of the National Gallery—a landscape of Turner's, and a portrait by Reynolds, in which she fancied a resemblance to her father.

"My last Sunday before term began was spent almost entirely with Esperanza. I accepted Martha's invitation to partake of her Sunday dinner, and sat at meat with dear old Benjamin for the first time in my life, though I had eaten many a meal with his worthy wife in the days when my legs reached a very little way below the table and my manners were in sore need of the good soul's supervision—happy childish days, before governess and lesson-books had appeared upon the scene of my life; days in which life was one long game of play, interrupted only by childish illnesses that were like bad dreams, troubled and indistinct patches on the fair foreground of the childish memory. The good Benjamin ate his roast beef in a deprecating and apologetic attitude, sitting, I fear, uncomfortably, on the edge of his chair. Esperanza ate about as much solid food as a singing bird might have done; but she looked stronger and in better health than on the night of the *séance*, and she looked almost happy. After the roast beef and apple-tart, I took her to an afternoon service at St. Paul's, where the organ-music filled her with rapture.

"'I shall come here every Sunday,' she said, as we left the cathedral.

"I entreated her not to go so far alone, and warned her that the streets of London were full of danger for youth and inexperience; but she laughed at my fears, assuring me that she had walked about the meadows and coppices round Besbery ever since she could remember, and no harm had ever befallen her, though there were hardly any people about. I told her that in London the people were the danger, and exacted her promise that she would never go beyond the immediate neighbourhood of Great Ormond Street by herself. I gave her permission to walk about Queen's Square, Guilford Street, and Mecklenburgh Square. The neighbourhood was quiet and respectable.

"'I am bound to obey you,' she answered meekly. 'I owe you so much gratitude for your goodness to me.'

"I protested against gratitude to *me*. The only friend to whom she owed anything was my dear old nurse.

"I had a great terror of the perils of the London streets for a girl of her appearance. It was not so much that she was beautiful, but because of a certain strangeness and exceptional character in her beauty which would be likely to attract attention and arouse curiosity. The dreamy look in the large violet eyes, the semi-transparent pallor which suggested an extreme fragility, the unworldliness of her whole aspect were calculated to appeal to the worst instincts of the prowling profligate. She had an air of helplessness which would invite persecution from the cowardly wretches who make the streets of a great city perilous for unprotected innocence.

"She was ready to promise anything that would please me.

"'I do not care if I never go out,' she said simply. 'The lady who lives in the drawing-room has a harmonium, and she has told me I may play upon it every day—all day long, when she is out; and she has a great many friends, and visits a good deal.'

"'Oh, but you must go out-of-doors for your health's sake!' I protested. 'Martha or Benjamin must go with you.'

"'They have no time to go out-of-doors till after dark, poor things! they are so busy; but they will take me for a walk sometimes of an evening. I shall make them go out, for their own sakes. You need not feel anxious about me; you are too kind to think of me at all.'

"I could not help feeling anxious about her. I felt as if I were responsible for everything that could assail or hurt her; that every hair of her head was a charge upon my conscience. Her health, her happiness, her talents and tastes and fancies—it was mine to care for all these. My *protégée*, Standish called her. In this farewell walk through the dull Sunday streets, in the dull

October twilight, it seemed as if she were much more than my *protégée*—my dearest, most sacred care, the purpose and the promise of my life.

"To-night we were to say good-bye. We were to have parted at the door in Great Ormond Street; but, standing on the doorstep, waiting for the opening of that inexorable door, which would swallow her up presently, like a tomb, I felt all at once that I could not sacrifice this last evening. Standish was dining out. There would only be loneliness and a roast chicken awaiting me at half-past seven. The chicken might languish, uneaten; the ghosts might have the dull, commonplace room; I would finish the evening with Martha's tea and toast, and hear Esperanza sing her favourite numbers of Handel and Mendelssohn, to the accompaniment of an ancient Stoddart piano, a relic of the schoolroom in my Suffolk home, the piano on which my mother took her first music-lesson.

"It was an evening in Elysium. A back parlour is sometimes large enough to contain paradise. I did not question my own heart, or analyze my beatific sensations. I ascribed at least half my happiness to Handel and Mendelssohn, and that feeling of exaltation which only sacred music can produce. There were no anxious questionings in my mind till after I had said good-bye to Esperanza—good-bye, till the third week in December—and had left the house. Those uneasy questionings were inspired by my dear old Martha, who opened the hall door for me, and said gravely, as I shook hands with her—

"'It would never do, Mr. George. I know what kind of lady your mother is, as well as anybody. It would never do.'

"I did not ask her what it was that would never do; but I carried a new sense of trouble and difficulty out into the autumn wind.

CHAPTER IX
"A WHITE STAR MADE OF MEMORY LONG AGO"

"'It would never do.' Those words of Martha's—so earnestly spoken by the kind soul who cared for me almost as tenderly as a mother cares for her own—haunted me all through the rapid run to Cambridge, walked the quadrangles of Trinity with me, tramped the Trumpington Road upon my shoulders, like that black care which sits behind the traveller. 'It would never do.' No need to ask my good Martha for the meaning of that emphatic assertion. I knew what shape her thoughts had taken as she watched me sitting by the little square piano—the old, old piano, with such a thin, tinkling sound—listening to that seraphic voice, and looking at that delicate profile and exquisite colouring of faintly flushed cheek, lifted eye, and shadowy hair. My old nurse had surprised my secret almost before I knew it myself; but, by the time I was back in my shabby ground-floor sitting-room at Trinity, I knew as well as Martha knew that I had let myself fall deep in love with a girl whom I could never marry with my mother's approbation. I might take my own way in life and marry the girl I loved; but to do so would be to forfeit my mother's affection, to make myself an outcast from her house.

"'I know what kind of a lady your mother is,' said Martha, in her valedictory address.

"Was I, her son, likely to be ignorant of the mother's character, or unable to gauge the strength of her prejudices—prejudices that seemed so much a part of her nature as to form a strong argument against Locke's assertion that there are no innate ideas? Indeed, in reading that philosopher's famous chapter, it always seemed to me, that if the average infant had to begin the A B C of life at the first letter, my mother must be a 'sport' or exception to the general rule, and must have been born with her brain richly stocked with family pride and social distinctions. In all the years I had lived with her I had never seen her unbend to a servant, or converse on equal terms with a tradesman. She had a full appreciation of the value of wealth when it was allied with good birth; but the millionaire manufacturer or the lucky speculator belonged to that outer circle of which she knew nothing, and of which she would believe no good.

"I was her only son; and she was a widow. I owed her more than most sons owe their mothers. I did not stand as number four or five in a family circle, taking my share in the rough and tumble of family life. My mother had been all in all to me; and I had been all in all to her. I had been her friend and companion from the time I was able to understand the English language, the recipient of all her ideas, her likes and dislikes—from the early stage when the childish mind unconsciously takes shape and bent from the mind of the parent the child loves best. From my seventh year I was fatherless, and all that is sacred and sweet in home life began and ended for me with the word mother.

"My mother was what Gerald Standish called 'a masterful woman,' a woman to whom it was natural to direct and initiate the whole business of life. My father was her opposite in temperament,—irresolute, lymphatic; and I think he must have handed her the reins of home government before their honeymoon was over. I remember him just well enough to remember that he left the direction of his life wholly to her; that he deferred to her judgment, and studied her feelings in every detail of his existence; and that he obviously adored her. I don't think he cared very much for me, his only child. I can recall no indication of warmth of feeling on his part, only a placid indifference, as of one whose affection was concentrated upon a single object, and whose heart had no room for any other image. He spoke of me as 'the boy,' and looked at me occasionally with an air of mild wonder, as if I were somebody else's son, whose growth took him by surprise. I never remember his expressing any opinion about me, except that I had grown since he looked at me last.

"His feeling about me being thus tepid, it was hardly surprising that he should make what many people have called an unjust will. I have never disputed its justice, for I loved my mother too much to complain of the advantages of power and status which that will gave her.

"She was an heiress, and her money had cleared my father's estate from heavy encumbrances, and no doubt he remembered this when providing for her future. He was her senior by five and twenty years, and foresaw a long widowhood for her.

"The entail ended in his own person, so he was free to dispose of his property as he liked. He left my mother tenant for life; and he left me five hundred a year, chargeable upon the estate, which income was only to begin when I came of age. Till my one-and-twentieth birthday I was dependent upon my mother for everything.

"I told myself that I had to cut my own path in life, and that I must be the architect of my own fortune.

"My mother's income, under her marriage settlement, was considerable, and this, in addition to a rent-roll of between two and three thousand a year, made her a rich woman.

"Assuredly I was not in a position to make an imprudent marriage, since my power to maintain a wife and family in accord with my own ideas of a gentleman's surroundings must depend for a considerable time upon my mother's liberality. I had made up my mind to go to the Bar, and I knew how slow and arduous is the road to success in that branch of the legal profession; but far nearer than mere questions of interest was the obligation which filial love laid upon me. My mother had given me the devotion of years, had made me the chief object of her thoughts and her hopes, and I should be an ungrateful wretch if I were to disappoint her. I knew, alas! that upon this very question of marriage she cherished a project that it would distress her to forego, and that there was a certain Lady Emily whom I was intended to marry, the daughter of a nobleman who had been my father's most intimate friend, and for whom my mother had a greater regard than for any of our neighbours.

"Knowing this, and wishing with all my heart to do my duty as a son to the best of mothers, I could but echo Martha's solemn words—

"'It would never do.'

"No, 'it would never do.' The seraphic voice, the spiritual countenance, the appealing helplessness, which had so moved my pity, must be to me as a dream from which I had awakened. Esperanza's fate must rest henceforward with herself, aided by honest Martha Blake, and helped, through Martha, from my purse. I must never see her again. No word had been spoken, no hint had been given of the love which it was my bounden duty to conquer and forget. I could contemplate the inevitable renunciation with a clear conscience.

"I worked harder in that term than I had worked yet, and shut my door against all the allurements of undergraduate friends and all the pleasures of university life. I was voted churlish and a muff; but I found my books the best cure for an unhappy love; and though the image of Miss Campbell was oftener with me than the learned shade of Newton or the later ghost of Whewell, I contrived to do some really good work.

"My mother and I wrote to each other once a week. She expected me to send her a budget of gossip and opinion, and it was only in this term that I began to feel a difficulty in filling two sheets of note-paper with my niggling penmanship. For the first time in my life, I found myself sitting, pen in hand, with nothing to say to my mother. I could not write about Esperanza, or the passionate yearning which I was trying to outlive. I could hardly expatiate upon my mathematical studies to a woman who, although highly cultivated, knew nothing of mathematics. I eked out my letter as best I could, with a laboured criticism upon a feeble novel which I had idly skimmed in an hour of mental exhaustion.

"I looked forward apprehensively to my home-going in December, fearing that some change in my outward aspect might betray the mystery of my heart. The holiday, once so pleasant, would be long and dull. The shooting would afford some relief perhaps, and I made up my mind to tramp the plantations all day long. At Cambridge I had shirked physical exercise; in Suffolk I would walk down my sorrow.

"A letter from my mother, which reached me early in December, put an end to these resolves. She had been somewhat out of health all through November; and her local medical man, who was old and *passé*, had only tormented her with medicines which made her worse. She had therefore decided, at Miss Marjorum's earnest desire, upon spending my vacation in London; and Jebson, her trusty *major domo*, had been up to town, and had found her delightful lodgings on the north side of Hyde Park. She would await me, not at Fendyke, but in Connaught Place.

"Connaught Place—within less than an hour's walk of Great Ormond Street! My heart beat fast and furiously at the mere thought of that propinquity. Martha's latest letter had told me that all attempts at finding a situation for my *protégée* had so far been without result. Martha and her charge had visited all the agencies for the placing of governesses and companions, and no agent had succeeded in placing Esperanza. Her education was far below the requirements of the least exacting employer. She knew very little French, and no German; she played exquisitely, but she played by ear; of the theory of music she knew hardly anything. Her father, an enthusiast and a dreamer, had filled her with ideas, but had taught her nothing that would help her to earn a living.

"'Don't you fret about her, Mr. George,' wrote Martha. 'As long as I have a roof over my head, she can make her home with me. Her bite and sup makes hardly any difference in the week's expenses. I'm only sorry, for her sake, that she isn't clever enough to get into a nice family in some pretty country house, like Fendyke. It's a dull life for her here—a back parlour to live in, and two old people for her only companions.'

"I thought of the small dark parlour in the Bloomsbury lodging-house, the tinkling old piano, the dull grey street; a weary life for a girl of poetic temperament reared in the country. That letter of Martha's, and the fact of being within an easy walk of Great Ormond Street, broke down my resolution of the last two months. I called upon Martha and her charge on the morning after I left Cambridge. I thought Esperanza looked wan and out of health, and could but mark how the pale, sad face flushed and brightened at sight of me. We were alone for a few minutes, while Martha interviewed a butcher, and I seized the opportunity. I said I feared she was not altogether happy. Only unhappy in being a burden to my friends, she told me. She was depressed by finding her own uselessness. Hundreds of young women were earning their living as governesses, but no one would employ her.

"'No lady will even give me a trial,' she said. 'I'm afraid I must look very stupid.'

"'You look very lovely,' I answered hotly. 'They want a commoner clay.'

"I implored her to believe that she was no burden to Martha or to me. If she could be content to live that dull and joyless life, she was at least secure of a safe and respectable home; and if she cared to carry on her education, something might be done in the way of masters; or she might attend some classes in Harley Street, or elsewhere.

"She turned red and then pale, and I saw tears trembling on her long auburn lashes.

"'I am afraid I am unteachable,' she faltered, with downcast eyes. 'Kind ladies at Besbery tried to teach me; but it was no use. My mind always wandered. I could not keep my thoughts upon the book I was reading, or on what they told me. Miss Grimshawe, who wanted to help me, said I was incorrigibly idle and atrociously obstinate. But, indeed, it was not idleness or obstinacy that kept me from learning. I could not force myself to think or to remember. My thoughts would only go their own way; and I cared for nothing but music, or for the poetry my father used to read to me sometimes of an evening. I am afraid Miss Grimshawe was right, and that I ought to be a dressmaker.'

"I glanced at the hands which lay loosely clasped upon the arm of the chair in which she was sitting. Such delicately tapering fingers were never meant for the dressmaker's workroom. The problem of Esperanza's life was not to be solved that way.

"I did not remain long on this first morning; but I went again two days afterwards, and again, until it came to be every day. Martha grumbled and warned me of my danger, and of the wrong done to Esperanza, if I were to make her care for me.

"'I don't think there's much fear of that,' added Martha. 'She's too much in the clouds. It's you I'm afraid of. You and me knows who mamma wants you to marry, don't us, Mr. George?'

"I could not gainsay Martha upon this point. Lady Emily and I had ridden the same rocking-horse; she riding pillion with her arms clasped round my waist, while I urged the beast to his wildest pace. We had taken tea out of the same toy tea-things—her tea-things—and before I was fifteen years of age my mother told me that she was pleased to see I was so fond of Emily, and hoped that she and I would be husband and wife some day, in the serious future, just as we were little lovers now in the childish present.

"I remember laughing at my mother's speech, and thinking within myself that Emily and I hardly realized my juvenile idea of lovers. The romantic element was entirely wanting in our association. When I talked of Lady Emily, later, to Gerald Standish, I remember I described her as 'a good sort,' and discussed her excellent qualities of mind and temper with an unembarrassed freedom which testified to a heart that was at peace.

"I felt more mortified than I would have cared to confess at Martha's blunt assurance that Esperanza was too much in the clouds to care about me; and it may be that this remark of my old nurse's gave just the touch of pique that acted as a spur to passion. I know that after two or three afternoons in Great Ormond Street, I felt that I loved this girl as I could never love again, and that henceforward it would be impossible for me to contemplate the idea of life without her. The more fondly I loved her, the less demonstrative I became, and my growing reserve threw dust in the elderly eyes that watched us. Martha believed that her warning had taken effect, and she so far confided in my discretion as to allow me to take Esperanza for lamp-lit walks in the Bloomsbury squares, after our cosy tea-drinking in the little back parlour. The tea-drinking and the walk became an institution. Martha's rheumatics had made walking exercise impossible for her during the last month. Benjamin was fat and lazy.

"'If I didn't let the poor child go out with you, she'd hardly get a breath of fresh air all the winter. And I know that I can trust you, Mr. George,' said Martha.

"'Yes, you can trust me,' answered I.

"She might trust me to breathe no word of evil into the ear of her I loved. She could trust me to revere the childlike innocence which was my darling's highest charm. She could trust me to be loyal and true to Esperanza. But she could not trust me to be worldly-wise, or to sacrifice my own happiness to filial affection. The time came when I had to set my love for Esperanza against my duty to my mother and my own interests. Duty and interest kicked the beam.

"Oh, those squares! those grave old Bloomsbury squares, with their formal rows of windows, and monotonous iron railings, and stately doorways, and clean doorsteps, and enclosures of trees, whose blackened branches showed leafless against the steely sky of a frosty evening! What groves or streams of paradise could be fairer to us two than the dull pavements which we paced arm-in-arm in the wintry greyness, telling each other those thoughts and fancies which seemed in their intuitive sympathy to mark us for predestined life-companions. Her thoughts were childishly expressed sometimes; but it seemed to me always as if they were only my thoughts in a feminine guise. Nothing that she said ever jarred upon me; and her ignorance of the world and all its ways suggested some nymph or fairy reared in the seclusion of woodland or ocean cave. I thought of Endymion, and I fancied that his goddess could have been scarcely less of the earth than this fair girl who walked beside me, confiding in me with a childlike faith.

"One night I told her that I loved her. We had stayed out later than usual. The clock of St. George's Church was striking nine, and in the shadowy quiet of Queen's Square my lips met hers in love's first kiss. How shyly and how falteringly she confessed her own secret, so carefully guarded till that moment.

"'I never thought you could care for a poor girl like me,' she said; 'but I loved you from the first. Yes, almost from the very first. My heart seemed frozen after my father's death, and your voice was the first that thawed it. The dull, benumbed feeling passed away, and I knew that I had some one living to love and care for and think about as I sat alone. I had a world of new thoughts to interweave with the music I love.'

"'Ah, that music, Esperanza! I am almost jealous of music when I see you so moved and influenced by it.'

"'Music would have been my only consolation if you had not cared for me,' she answered simply.

"'But I do care for you, and I want you to be my wife, now at once—as soon as we can be married.'

"I talked about an immediate marriage before the registrar. But, willing as she was to be guided by me in most things, she would not consent to this.

"'It would not seem like marriage to me,' she said, "if we did not stand before the altar.'

"'Well, it shall be in a church, then; only we shall have to wait longer. And I must go back to Cambridge at the end of this week. I must get an exeat, and come up to London on our wedding-day, and take you home in the evening. I shall have a quiet home ready for my darling, far from the ken of dons and undergraduates, but within an easy distance of the 'Varsity.'

"I explained to her that our marriage must be a secret till I came of age next year, or till I could find a favourable opportunity of breaking the fact to my mother.'

"'Will she mind? Will she be angry?' asked Esperanza.

"'Not when she comes to know you, dear love.'

"Although I knew my mother's strong character, I was infatuated enough to believe what I said. Where was the heart so stony that would not warm to that fair and gentle creature? Where the pride so stubborn which that tender influence could not bend?

"I had the banns put up at the church of St. George the Martyr, assured that Martha's rheumatism and Benjamin's lethargic temper would prevent either of them attending the morning service on any of the three fateful Sundays. If Martha went to church at all, she crept there in the evening, after tea. She liked the gaslights and the evening warmth, the short prayers, and the long sermon, and she met her own class among the congregation. I felt tolerably safe about the banns.

"Had my mother been in good health, it would have been difficult for me to spend so many of my evenings away from home; but the neuralgic affection which had troubled her in Suffolk had not been subjugated by the great Dr. Gull's treatment, and she passed a good deal of her life in her own rooms and in semi-darkness, ministered to by a lady who had been a member of our household ever since my father's death, and whose presence had been the only drawback to my home happiness.

"This lady was my mother's governess—Miss Marjorum—a woman of considerable brain power, wide knowledge of English and German literature, and a style of pianoforte playing which always had the effect of cold water down my back. And yet Miss Marjorum played correctly. She introduced no discords into that hard, dry music, which seemed to me to have been written expressly for her hard and precise finger-tips, bony knuckles, and broad, strong hand, with a thumb which she boasted of as resembling Thalberg's. In a difficult and complicated movement Miss Marjorum's thumb worked wonders. It was ubiquitous; it turned under and over, and rapped out sharp staccato notes in the midst of presto runs, or held rigid semibreves while the active fingers fired volleys of chords, shrilled out a six-bar shake, or raced the bass with lightning triplets. In whatever entanglement of florid ornament Liszt or Thalberg had disguised a melody, Miss Marjorum's thumb could search it out and drum it into her auditors.

"Miss Marjorum was on the wrong side of fifty. She had a squat figure and a masculine countenance, and her voice was deep and strong, like the voice of a man. She dressed with a studious sobriety in dark cloth or in grey alpaca, according to the seasons, and in the evening she generally wore plaid poplin, which ruled her square, squat figure into smaller squares. I have observed an affinity between plain people and plaid poplin.

"Miss Marjorum was devoted to my mother; and antagonistic as her nature was to me in all things, and blighting as was her influence upon the fond dream of my youth, I am bound to record that she was conscientious in carrying out her own idea of duty. Her idea of duty unhappily included no indulgence for youthful impulses, and she disapproved of every independent act of mine.

"My evening absences puzzled her.

"'I wonder you can like to be out nearly every evening when your mother is so ill,' she remarked severely, on my return to Connaught Place after that glimpse of paradise in Queen Square.

"'If I could be of any use to my mother by staying at home, you may be sure I should not be out, Miss Marjorum,' I replied, rather stiffly.

"'It would be a satisfaction to your mother to know you were under her roof, even when she is obliged to be resting quietly in her own room.'

"'Unfortunately my mathematical coach lives under another roof, and I have to accommodate myself to his hours.'

"This was sophistication; but it was true that I read mathematics with an ex-senior wrangler in South Kensington every other day.

"'Do you spend *every* evening with your coach?' asked Miss Marjorum, looking up suddenly from her needlework, and fixing me with her cold grey eye.

"'Certainly not. You know the old saw—"All work and no play——"'

"'And how do you amuse yourself when you are not at South Kensington? I did not think you knew many people in London.'

"'That is because I know very few people whom you know. My chief friends are the friends of my college life—not the worthy bucolics of Suffolk.'

Miss Marjorum sighed, and went on with her sewing. She delighted in the plainest of plain work—severest undergarments of calico or flannel.

She had taken upon herself to supply my mother's poorer cottage-tenants with under-clothing—a very worthy purpose; but I could not help wishing she had deferred a little more to the universal sense of beauty in her contributions to the cottagers' wardrobes. Surely those prison-like garments must have appalled their recipients. My inexperienced eye noted only their ugliness in shape and coarseness of texture. I longed for a little trimming, a softer quality of flannel.

"'I am afraid they must hurt the people who get them,' I said one day, when Miss Marjorum exhibited her bale of flannel underwear.

"'They are delightfully warm, and friction promotes circulation and maintains the health of the skin,' she replied severely. 'I don't know what *more* you would have.'

"It irked me not a little to note Miss Marjorum's suspicious air when she discussed my evening occupations, for I knew she had more influence over my mother than any one living, and I fancied that she would not scruple to use that influence against me. I had lost her friendship long ago by childish rudenesses, which I looked back upon with regret, but which I could not obliterate from her memory by the studious civilities of later years.

"I went back to Cambridge, and my mother and her devoted companion left Connaught Place for Brighton, Dr. Gull having strongly recommended sea-air, after exhausting his scientific means in the weary battle with nerve pain. It was a relief to me, when I thought of Esperanza, to know that Miss Marjorum was fifty miles away from Great Ormond Street. Those suspicious glances and prying questions of hers had frightened me.

"*When* I thought of Esperanza!—when was she not the centre and circumference of my thoughts? I worked hard; missed no lecture; neglected no opportunity; for I had made up my mind to win the game of life off my own bat; but Esperanza's image was with me whatever I was doing. I think I mixed up her personality in an extraordinary fashion with the higher mathematics. She perched like a fairy upon every curve, or slid sylph-like along every line. I weighed her, and measured her, and calculated the doctrine of chances about her. She became in my mind the ruling, and to common eyes, invisible spirit of the science of quantity and number.

"Could this interval between the asking in church and my wedding-day be any other than a period of foolish dreaming, of fond confusion and wandering thoughts? I was not twenty-one, and I was about to take a step which would inevitably offend my only parent, the only being to whom I stood indebted for care and affection. In the rash hopefulness of a youthful passion, I made sure of being ultimately forgiven; but, hopeful as I was, I knew it might be some time before I could obtain pardon. In the meanwhile,

I had an income which would suffice for a youthful *ménage*. I would find a quiet home for Esperanza at one of the villas on the Grandchester Road till I had taken my degree, and then I should have to begin work in London. Indeed, I had fixed in my own mind upon a second-floor in Martha's roomy old house, which would be conveniently near the Temple, where I might share a modest set of chambers with a Cambridge friend. In the deep intoxication of my love-dream, Great Ormond Street seemed just the most delightful spot in which to establish the cosy home I figured to myself. It would be an infinite advantage to live under my dear old nurse's roof, and to know that she would watch over my girl-wife while I sat waiting for briefs in my dingy chambers, or reading law with an eminent junior.

"I had asked Esperanza on the night of our betrothal whether she thought we could live upon five hundred a year. A ripple of laughter preluded her reply.

"'Dear George, do you know what my father's income was?' she asked. 'Sixty-five pounds a year. He paid fifteen pounds a year for our cottage and garden—such a dear old garden—and we had to live and clothe ourselves upon the other fifty pounds. He was very shabby sometimes, poor darling; but we were always happy. Though I seem so helpless in getting my own living, I think I could keep house for you, and not waste your money. Five hundred a year! Why, you are immensely rich!'

"I told her that I should be able to add to our income by the time we had been married a few years, and then we would have a house in the country, and a garden, and a pair of ponies for her to drive, and cows and poultry, and all the things that women love. What a happy dream it was, and how the sweet face brightened under the lamplight as she listened to me.

"'I want nothing but your love,' she said; 'nothing. I am not afraid of poverty.'

"The three weeks were gone. I got an exeat, and went up to London by an early train. I had directed Esperanza to meet me at the church, whose doors we had so often passed together in our evening walks, and where we had knelt side by side one Sunday evening. She was to take Martha to church with her; but not till the last moment, not till they were at the church door, was she to tell my old nurse what was going to happen, lest an idea of duty to the mother should induce her to betray the son.

"The air was crisp and bright, and the wintry landscape basked in the wintry sun between Cambridge and Stratford; but the dull greyness of our metropolitan winter wrapped me round when I left Bishopsgate Street, and there was a thin curtain of fog hanging over my beloved Bloomsbury when my hansom rattled along the sober old-world streets to the solid Georgian church. I sprang from the cab as if I had worn Mercury's sandals, told the man to wait, ran lightly up the steps, pushed back the heavy door and entered the dark temple, hushed and breathless. How solemn and cold and ghostly the church looked, how grey and pale the great cold windows. The fog seemed thicker here than in the streets outside; and the dreary fane was empty.

"I looked at my watch. Twenty minutes to eleven. I had entreated her to be at the church at least ten minutes before the hour; and I felt bitterly disappointed that she had not anticipated the appointment.

"Her last letter was three days old. Could she be ill? could any evil thing have happened? I hurried back to the church door, intending to get into my cab and drive to Ormond Street. I changed my mind before I had crossed the threshold. I might miss her on the way—drive by one street while she and Martha were walking in another. Again, there was something undignified in a bridegroom rushing off in search of his bride. My place was to wait in the church. I had seen a good many weddings in our parish church in Suffolk, and I knew that the bride was almost always late. Yet, in spite of this experience, I had expected my bride in advance of the appointed time. She had no wreath of orange-blossoms, no bridal veil to adjust, no doting mother, or sister bridesmaids to flurry and hinder her under the pretence of helping. She had no carriage to wait for. Her impatience to see me after nearly three weeks should have brought her to the church earlier than this.

"Then I remembered Martha. No doubt she was waiting for Martha. That good soul was interviewing the butcher, or adjusting her Paisley shawl, while I was fretting and fuming in the church. I had no best man to reason with my impatience and keep up my spirits. My best man was to be the parish clerk, and he had not yet appeared upon the scene. I saw a pew-opener creeping about, a pew-opener in the accustomed close black bonnet and sober apparel. Esperanza's bridesmaid! Martha would have to give her away.

"I took a turn round the church, looked at the monuments, and even stood still to read a tablet here and there, and knew no more of the inscription after I had read it than if it had been in choice Assyrian.

"I opened the heavy door and went out on the steps, and stood watching a stray cab or a stray pedestrian, dimly visible through the thickening fog. I looked at my watch every other minute, between anger and despair. It was five minutes to eleven. The curate who was to marry us passed me on the steps and went into the church, unsuspecting that I was to be the chief actor in the ceremony. I stood looking along the street, in the only direction in which my bride was to be expected, and my heart sickened as the slow minutes wore themselves out, till it was nearly a quarter-past eleven.

"I could endure this no longer. My hansom was waiting on the opposite side of the street. I lifted my finger, and signed to the driver to come over to me. There was nothing for it but to go to Great Ormond Street, and discover the cause of delay.

"Before the man could climb into his seat and cross the road, a brougham drove sharply up to the church steps—a brougham of dingy aspect, driven by a man whose livery branded him as a flyman.

"I was astonished at the fly, but never doubted that it brought me my dear love, and my heart was light again, and I ran to greet her with a welcoming smile.

"The carriage door was sharply opened from within, and my mother stepped out and stood before me, tall and grave, in her neat dark travelling dress, her fine features sharp and clear in the wintry gloom.

"'Mother!' I exclaimed aghast.

"'I know I am not the person you expected, George,' she said quietly. 'Badly as you have behaved to me, I am sorry for your disappointment.'

"'Where is Esperanza?' I cried, unheeding my mother's address.

"It was only afterwards that her words came back to me—in that long dull afterwards when I had leisure to brood over every detail in this agonizing scene.

"'She is safe, and in good hands, and she is where you will never see her again.'

"'That's a lie!' I cried. 'If she is among the living, I will find her. If she is dead, I will follow her.'

"'You are violent and unreasonable; but I suppose your romantic infatuation must excuse you. When you have read this letter, you will be calmer, I hope.'

"She gave me a letter in Esperanza's writing. We had moved a few paces from the church steps while we talked. I read the letter, walking slowly along the street, my mother at my side.

> "'DEAREST,
>
> "'I am going away. I am not to be your wife. It was a happy dream, but a foolish one. I should have ruined your life. That has been made clear to me; I love you far too dearly to be your enemy. You will never see me

again. Don't be unhappy about me. I shall be well cared for. I am going very far away; but if it were to the farthest end of the earth, and if I were to live a hundred years, I should never cease to love you, or learn to love you less.

"'Good-bye for ever,

"'ESPERANZA.'

"'I know whose hand is in this,' I said,—'Miss Marjorum.'

"'Miss Marjorum is my true and loyal friend, and yours too, though you may not believe it.'

"'Whoever it may be who has stolen my love away from me, that person is my dire and deadly foe. Whether the act is yours or hers, it is the act of my bitterest enemy, and I shall ever so remember it. Look here, mother, let there be no misunderstanding between you and me. I love this girl better than my life. Whatever trick you have played upon her, whatever cajoleries you and Miss Marjorum have brought to bear upon her, whatever false representations you may have made, appealing to her unselfishness against her love, you have done that which will wreck your son's life unless you can undo it.'

"'I have saved my son from the shipwreck his own folly would have made of his life,' my mother answered calmly. 'I have seen what these unequal marriages come to—before the wife is thirty.'

"'It would be no unequal marriage. The girl I love is a lady.'

"'A village organist's daughter, by her own confession totally without education. A pretty, delicate young creature with a certain surface refinement, I grant you; but do you think that would stand the wear and tear of life, or counterbalance your humiliation when people asked questions about your wife's antecedents and belongings? People, even the politest people, *will* ask those questions, George. My dear, dear boy, the thing you were to have done to-day would have been utter ruin to your social existence for the next fifty years. You will never be rich enough or great enough to live down such a marriage.'

"'Don't preach to me,' I cried savagely. 'You have broken my heart. Surely that is enough for you.'

"I broke away from her as she laid her hand upon my arm—such a shapely hand in a dark grey glove. I remembered even in that moment of anguish and of anger how my dear love had often walked by my side, gloveless, shabbier than a milliner's apprentice. No, she was not of my mother's world; no more was Titania. She belonged to the realm of romance and *féerie*; not to Belgravia or Mayfair.

"I ran back to the spot where the hansom still waited for me, jumped in, and told the man to drive to Great Ormond Street. I left my mother standing on the pavement, to find her way back to her carriage as she could, to go where she would.

"I knocked at the lodging-house door loud enough to wake the Seven Sleepers. I pushed past the scared maid-servant, and dashed into Martha's parlour. She was sitting with her spectacles on her nose poring over a tradesman's book, and with other books of the same kind on the table before her.

"'Martha, this is your doing,' I said. 'You betrayed me to my mother!'

"'Oh, Mr. George, forgive your old nurse that loves you as if you were her own flesh and blood. I only did my duty by you and my mistress. It would never have done.'

"She called me 'dear,' as in the old nursery days. Tears were streaming down her withered cheeks.

"'It was you, then?'

"'Yes, it was me, Mr. George, leastways me and Benjamin. We talked it over a long time before he wrote the letter to my mistress at Brighton. Sarah came home from church on Sunday dinner-time. The drawing-rooms were dining out, and the second floor is empty, so there was nothing to hinder Sarah's going to church. She came home at dinner-time, and told me you and Esperanza Campbell had been asked in church—for the third time. You might have knocked me down with a feather. I never thought she could be so artful. I talked it over with Benjamin, and he posted a letter that night.'

"'And Miss Marjorum came up from Brighton next morning, and came to see Esperanza?'

"'How did you know that, Mr. George?'

"'I know Miss Marjorum.'

"'Yes, it was Miss Marjorum that came. She asked to see Esperanza alone, and they were shut up together for over an hour, and then the bell was rung, and Miss Marjorum told the girl to pack up Miss Campbell's things, bring her box down to the hall, and when she had done that, to fetch a four-wheeler. Sarah was nearly as upset as I was, but she and I packed the things between us—such a few things, poor child—and carried the box downstairs, and I waited in the hall while Sarah ran for the cab. And presently Esperanza came out of the parlour with Miss Marjorum, and put on her hat and jacket, and then came to bid me good-bye.

"'She put her arms round my neck and kissed me; and though I had done my duty by you and your ma, Mr. George, I felt like Judash. "It was right of you to tell," she said; "it was only right—for his sake," and Miss Marjorum hurried her down the steps and into the cab before she could say another word. I do believe the poor dear child gave you up without a murmur, Mr. George, because she knew that it would have been your ruin to marry her.'

"'Bosh! That had been drummed into her by Miss Marjorum. You have done me the worst turn you ever did any one in your life, Martha; and yet I thought if there was anybody in the world I could trust it was you. Where did the cab go—do you know that?'

"'Charing Cross Station. I heard Miss Marjorum give the order.'"

CHAPTER X
"AND THAT UNREST WHICH MEN MISCALL DELIGHT"

Allan went back to Matcham sobered by grief, and longing for the comfort his betrothed could give him, the comfort of sympathy and gentle words, the deeper comfort in the assurance of her love.

Suzette looked very pale in her black frock when Allan appeared at Marsh House after his bereavement. They stood side by side in the grey light of a hopelessly dull day, finding but little speech in the sadness of this first meeting.

"My darling, you have been grieving for my grief," he said tenderly, looking into the dark eyes, noting the tired look as of many tears, the sharper line of the cheek, the settled pallor, where a lovely carmine had been wont to come and go like warm light.

"My dearest, you have lost all your roses—and for my sake. For me those dear eyes have known sleepless nights, those lovely cheeks have grown pinched and pale."

"Do you think that I could help being sorry for you, Allan?" she murmured, with downcast eyelids.

"You had no other cause for sorrow, I hope?"

"No, no; only in every life there are saddening intervals. I was sorry for your sake—sorry that I was never to see your father again. I liked him so much, Allan. And then somehow I got into a low-spirited way, and old Dr. Podmore gave me a tonic which made my head ache. I don't know that it had any other effect."

"Suzette, it was cruel of you not to tell me that you were ill."

"Oh, I was not to say ill. Why should I worry you about such nonsense? I was only below par. That is what Dr. Podmore called it. But please don't talk about me, Allan. Talk to me of yourself and of your poor mother. She is coming to stay with you, I hope?"

"Yes, she is coming to me next week. How is Mrs. Wornock? Do you go to her as much as ever?"

"Almost as much. She seems so dependent upon me for companionship, poor soul. I am the only girl she has taken to—as people say."

"What a wise woman to choose the most charming girl in the world."

"If you said in the Matcham world, it would not be a stupendous compliment."

"Nay, I mean the world. I challenge the universe to produce me a second Suzette. And Geoffrey, your violin player, has he been much at home?"

"Not very much. Please don't call him my violin player. I have not played a single accompaniment for him since you objected. I have been very dutiful."

"Don't talk of duty. It is love that I want, love without alloy; love which, being full of foolishness itself, can forgive a lover's baseless jealousy."

"Allan, have I ever been unforgiving?"

"No, you have borne with my tempers. You have been all that is kind and sweet—but I sometimes wish you would be angry with me. Would that there were a girl in Matcham handsome enough to admit of your jealousy! How desperately I would flirt with that girl!"

Her wan smile was not encouraging.

"Is he still as devoted to his fiddle? Does he talk of Tartini, Spontini, de Beriot, as other men talk of Salisbury or Gladstone?"

"I have seen very little of him; but he is a fanatic about music. He inherits his mother's passion."

"His poor mother," sighed Allan.

"She is so fond of you—almost as fond as she is of her own son."

"That's not possible, Suzie."

"Well, the son must be first, of course; but, indeed, she is very fond of you, Allan."

"Dear soul, it is for old sake's sake. I'll tell you her poor little innocent secret, Suzie. You, who are the other half of my soul, have a right to know all things which gravely interest me. Only you must be discretion itself; and you must never breathe a word of Mrs. Wornock's story to my mother."

And then he sat down by her side in the comfortable corner by the old-fashioned fireplace, fenced off from all the outer world by a Japanese screen, on which Choti and an army of smaller devils grinned and capered against a black satin background, and he told her tenderly, but only in outline, the story of his father's first love, and Esperanza's all-too-willing sacrifice.

"It was generous—but a mistake," he said in conclusion. "She gave up her own happiness, dashed away the cup of joy when it was at her lips. She was nobly unselfish, and she spoilt two lives. Such sacrifices never answer."

"Do you really believe that, Allan?" asked Suzette, looking at him with a startling intensity.

"I really do. I have never known a case in which self-surrender of that kind has ended well. A man and woman who love each other should be true to each other and their mutual love. All worldly considerations should be as naught. If a man truly loves a beggar-girl, let him marry her; and don't let the beggar-girl jilt him because she thinks he would do better by marrying a duchess."

"But if two people love each other—who are otherwise bound and fettered, who cannot be happy without breaking older ties——"

"Ah, that is a different thing. Honour comes into the question, and there must be sacrifices. This world would be a pandemonium if inclination went before honour. I am talking of love weighed against worldly wisdom, against poverty, against rank, race, wealth. You can understand now why Mrs. Wornock's heart went out to me from the beginning of our acquaintance—why she has accepted me almost as a second son."

Allan's Matcham friends were enthusiastic in their welcome, and cordial in their expressions of sympathy. It may be that the increase of means and importance which had come to him by his father's death was no small factor in the opinion of the village and its environs. A man who had an estate in Suffolk, and who lived at Matcham for his own pleasure, was a personage; and Matcham gossip did not fail to exaggerate the unseen Suffolk estate, and to talk of the Beechhurst property as a mere bagatelle, a windfall from a maternal uncle, hardly worth talking about, as compared with Fendyke and its vast acreage.

"Lady Emily has the house and home-farm for her life," Mrs. Mornington explained, with the privileged air of Allan's intimate friend; "but the bulk of the estate passes at once to Mr. Carew. My niece has done very well for herself, after all."

The last words, carelessly spoken, implied that in the first instance Mr. Carew had been rather a poor match for Miss Vincent.

"I suppose this sad event will delay the marriage?"

"For two or three months, perhaps. They were to have been married at midsummer, when Suzette will come of age; but she tells me she would not think of marrying Allan till at least half a year after his father's death. She talked of a year, but that would be simply absurd. The wedding can be as quiet as they like."

"Yes, of course," murmured assenting friends, sipping Mrs. Mornington's Ceylon tea, and despondently foreseeing the stern necessity of wedding presents, without even the poor compensation of champagne, ices, wedding-cake, and a crowd of fine gowns and new bonnets. They were to have positively no equivalent for their money.

Suzette had pleaded hard for a year's delay.

"It would be more respectful to him whom you have lost; and it would be more pleasing to your mother," she said.

"No, Suzette, my mother would rather see me happy than sacrifice my happiness to conventionality. Half a year is a long time for a man whose life seems a thing of shreds and patches, waiting the better fuller life that he longs for. I shall remember my dear father with no less affection; I shall no less regret his loss; when you and I are one. We can be married quietly at nine o'clock in the morning, before Matcham people have finished breakfast, with only your father and aunt, and my mother, for witnesses; and we can slip away from the station in the fresh September morning on the first stage of our journey to Como. Such a lovely journey at that season, Suzie! It will still be summer in Italy, and we can stay late in October, till the grapes are all gathered and the berceaus are getting bare, and then we can come back to Matcham to our own cosy fireside, and amuse ourselves with the arrangement of our house. It will be as new to me as it will be to you, Suzie, for only when you are its mistress will it be home."

Suzette could hardly withhold her consent, her lover being so earnest. It was settled that the marriage should take place early in September; and this being decided, the current of life flowed smoothly on, Allan spending more of his days at Marsh House, The Grove, and Discombe, than in his own house, except when Lady Emily was with him.

Discombe was by far the most delightful of these three houses in out-of-door weather, pleasant as were Mrs. Mornington's carefully tended grounds and shrubberies, her verandah and spacious conservatory.

The gardens at Discombe had that delicious flavour of the old world, and that absolute seclusion which can never be enjoyed in grounds that are within ear-shot of a high-road. At Discombe the long grass walks, the walls of ilex and of yew, the cypress avenues, and marble temples were isolated amidst surrounding woods, nearly a mile away from the traffic of everyday life. There was a sense of quiet and privacy here, compared with which Marsh House and the Grove were scarcely superior to the average villa in a newly developed suburb.

The seasons waxed and waned; the month of May, when the woodland walks round Discombe were white with the feathery bloom of the mountain ash, and golden with the scented blossoms of the yellow azalea; and June, which filled the woodland avenues with a flush of purple rhododendrons, masses of bloom, in an ascending scale of colour from the deep bass of darkest purple to the treble of palest lilac; and July, with her lap full of roses that made the gardens as brilliant as a picture by Alma Tadèma.

"I always tell the gardeners that if they give me roses I will forgive them all the rest," said Mrs. Wornock, when Allan complimented her upon her banquet of bloom; arches of roses, festoons of roses, temples built of roses, roses in beds and borders, everywhere.

"But your men are model gardeners; they neglect nothing."

In this paradise of flowers Allan and Suzette dawdled away two or three afternoons in every week. Discombe seemed to Allan always something of an enchanted palace—a place upon which there lay a glamour and a spell, a garden of sleep, a grove for woven paces and weaving hands, a spot haunted by sad sweet memories, ruled over by the genius of love, faithful in disappointment. Mrs. Wornock's personality gave an atmosphere of sadness to the house in which she lived, to the gardens in which she paced to and fro with slow, meditative steps; but it was not an unpleasing sadness, and it suited Allan's mood in this quiet summer of waiting, while grief for the loss of his father was still fresh in his mind.

Lady Emily came to Discombe on several occasions, and now that Mrs. Wornock's shyness had worn off—with all those agitations which were inevitable at a first meeting—the two women were very good friends. It was difficult for any one not to take kindly to Lady Emily Carew, and she on her side was fascinated by a nature so different from her own, and by that reserve force of genius which gave fire and pathos to Mrs. Wornock's playing.

Lady Emily listened with moistened eyes to the Sonata Pathetica, and Mrs. Wornock showed a cordial interest in the Blickling Park and Woodbastwick cows—which gave distinction to the Fendyke dairy farm.

"Pure white, with lovely black muzzles—and splendid milkers!" protested Lady Emily. "I was taught that thing you play, dear Mrs. Wornock; but my playing was never good for much, even when I was having two lessons a week from poor Sir Julius. He was only Mr. Benedict when he taught me, and he was almost young."

Geoffrey made meteoric appearances at Discombe during those quiet summer months, and his presence seemed to make everybody uncomfortable. There was a restlessness—a suppressed fever about him which made sensitive people nervous. Dearly though his mother loved him, and gladly as she welcomed his reappearance upon the scene of her life, she was always fluttered and anxious while he was under her roof.

His leave expired early in July, but instead of joining his regiment, which had returned to England, and was now quartered at York, he sent in his papers, without telling his mother or anybody else what he was doing, and he would not reconsider his decision when asked to do so by his colonel. He told his mother one morning at breakfast, in quite a casual way, that he had left the army.

"Oh, Geoffrey!" she exclaimed, with a shocked look.

"I hope you are not sorry. I thought it would please you for me to be my own master, able to spend more of my life with you."

"Dear Geoffrey, I am very glad on that account; but I'm afraid it is a selfish gladness. It was better for you to have a profession. Everybody told me so years ago, when I was so grieved at your going into the army."

"That is a way everybody has of saying smooth things. Well, mother, I am no longer a soldier. India was pleasant enough—there was a smack of adventure, a possibility of fighting—but I could not have endured garrison life in an English town. I would rather mope at home."

"Why should you mope, Geoff?"

"Yes, why? I am free to go east, west, north, and south. I suppose there need be no moping now?"

"But you will be often at home, won't you, dear? Or else I shall be no gainer by your leaving the army."

"Yes, I will be here as often, and as much as—as I can bear it."

He had risen from the breakfast-table, and was walking up and down the room, with that light careless step of his which seemed in perfect harmony with his tall slim figure. He was very pale, and his eyes were brighter than usual, and there was a quick restlessness in the smile that flashed across his face now and then.

"Do I bore you so much, Geoffrey?" his mother asked, with a wounded look.

"You bore me? No, no, no! Oh, surely you know how the land lies. Surely this fever cannot have been eating up my heart and my strength all this time without your eyes seeing, and your heart sympathizing. You *must* know that I love her."

"I feared as much, my poor Geoffrey."

No name had been spoken; yet mother and son understood each other.

"You feared! Great God, why should it be a reason for fear? Here am I, young, rich, my own master—and here is she as free as she is fair—free to be my wife to-morrow, except for this tie which is no tie—a foolish engagement to a man she never loved."

"Has she told you that?"

"Not she. Her lips are locked by an over-strained sense of honour. She will marry a man for whom she doesn't care a straw. She will be miserable all her life, or at best she will have missed happiness, and on her deathbed she will boast to her parish priest, 'I kept my word.' Poor pretty Puritan! She thinks it virtue to break my heart and grieve her own."

"You have told her of your love, Geoffrey?"

"Yes."

"That was dishonourable."

"No more than it was to love her. I am a lump of dishonour; I am made up of lies; but if she had an ounce of pluck, there need be no more falsehood. She has only to tell him the truth, the sad simple truth. 'I never loved you. I have let myself be persuaded into an engagement, but I never loved you.'"

"That would break Allan's heart."

"It would be bad to bear, no doubt, but not so bad as the gradual revelation that must come upon him in the years after marriage. She may be able to deceive him now—to delude him with the idea that she loves him; but how about the long winter evenings by their own fireside, and the dull nights when the rain is on the roof? A woman may hide her want of love before marriage; but, by Heaven, she can't hide it after! God help him when he finds that he has a victim, and not a wife!"

"Poor Allan! But how do you know she does not care for him—or that she cares for you?"

"How do I know that I live and breathe, that this is I?" touching himself, with an impatient tap of those light restless fingers. "I know it. I have known it more or less from the time we played those duets—the dawn of knowledge and of love. To know each other was to love. We were born for each other. Allan, with his shadowy resemblance to me, was only my forerunner, like the man one sees in the street, the man who reminds one of a dear friend, half an hour or so before we meet that very friend. Allan taught her to like the type. She never loved him. In me she recognizes the individual, fated to love her and to be loved by her."

"Dear Geoffrey, this is mere guess-work."

"No! It is instinct, intuition, dead certainty. I tell you—once, twice, a thousand times, if you like—she loves me, and she doesn't love him. Tax her with it, pluck out the heart of her mystery. This hollow sham—this simulacrum of love must not go on to marriage. Talk to her, as woman to woman, as mother to daughter. I tell you it must not go on. It is driving me mad."

"I will do what I can. Poor Allan! So good, so true-hearted!"

"Am I false-hearted or vile, mother? Why should Allan be all in all to you?"

"He is not all in all. You know you are the first, always the first in my heart; but I am deeply grieved for Allan. If what you tell me is true, he is doomed to be most unhappy. He is so fond of her. He has placed all his hopes of happiness upon his marriage—and they are to be married in little more than a month. It will be heartless to break it off."

"If it isn't broken off, there will be a tragedy. I will thrust myself between them at the altar. The lying words shall not be spoken. I would rather shoot him—or her—than that she should perjure herself, swear to love another while she loves only me!"

"Geoffrey, how do you know? How can you be sure——"

"Our hands have touched; our eyes have met. That is enough."

He walked out of the window to the garden, and from the garden to the stables, where he ordered his dog-cart. His servant kept a portmanteau always ready packed. He left Discombe within an hour of that conversation with his mother, and he was on his way to London before noon. The first intimation of his departure which Mrs. Wornock received was a note which she found on the luncheon-table.

> "I am off to the Hartz for a fortnight's tramp. Remember, something must be done to prevent this marriage. I shall return before the middle of August, and shall expect to find all settled.
>
> "Address Poste Restante, Hartzburg."

CHAPTER XI
"WHO KNOWS WHY LOVE BEGINS?"

The time was drawing near. The corn was cut and carried on many a broad sweep of hot chalky soil, and "summer's branding sun" had burnt up the thin grass on the wide bare down, where never shadow of tree or bush made a cool spot in the expanse of light and heat and dryness. The mysterious immemorial stones yonder on Salisbury Plain stood up against a background of cloudless blue; and the windows of the cathedral in the valley glittered and flashed in the sunshine. Only in the sober old close, and the venerable gardens of a bygone generation, within hedges that dead hands had planted, trees whose growth dead eyes had watched, was there coolness or shelter, or the gentle slumberous feeling of summer afternoon in its restful perfection.

Here, in an antique drawing-room, Mrs. Mornington and her niece were taking tea, after a morning with tailor and dressmaker.

"There never was such a girl for not-caringness as this girl of mine," said Mrs. Mornington, with a vexed air. "If it had not been for me, I don't think she would have had a new frock in her trousseau, and as she is a very prim personage about *lingerie*, and has a large stock of Parisian prettiness in that line, there would really have been nothing to buy."

"Rather a relief, I should think," laughed Mrs. Canon, who was giving them tea.

"A most delightful state of things," asserted Mrs. Sub-Dean, proud mother of half a dozen daughters, in which opinion agreed a county lady, also rich in daughters.

"Ah, you are all against me!" said Mrs. Mornington; "but there is a great pleasure in buying things, especially when one is spending somebody else's money."

"Poor papa!" sighed Suzette. "My aunt forgets that he is not Crœsus."

"Look at that girl's wretched pale face!" cried Mrs. Mornington. "Would any one think that she was going to be married to a most estimable young man, and the best match in the neighbourhood—except one?"

At those two last words, Suzette's cheeks flamed crimson, and the feminine conclave looking at her felt she was being cruelly used by this strong-minded aunt of hers.

"I don't think the nicest girls are ever very keen about their trousseau," said the county lady, with a furtive glance at a buxom freckled daughter, who had lately become engaged, and who had already begun to discuss house-linen and frocks, with a largeness of ideas that alarmed her parents.

"Yes; but there is a difference between caring too much and not caring at all. Suzette would be married in that white gingham she is wearing to-day, if I would let her."

"Pray don't teaze people about my frocks, auntie. If you can't find something more interesting to talk about, we had better go away," said Suzette, with a pettishness which was quite unlike her; but it must be owned that to be made the object of a public attack in feminine convocation was somewhat exasperating.

Mrs. Mornington was not to be put down. She went on talking of frocks, though one of the daughters of the house carried Suzette off to the garden—an act of real Christian charity, if she had not spoilt her good work by beginning to talk of Suzette's lover.

"I can quite fancy your aunt must be rather boring sometimes," she said. "But *do* tell me about Mr. Carew. I thought him so nice the other day at the flower-show, when you introduced him to me."

"What can I tell you about him? You have seen him—and I am glad you thought him nice."

"Yes; but one wants to know more. One wants to know what he is like—from your point of view."

"But how could you see him from my point of view? That's impossible."

"True! A casual acquaintance could never see him as he appears to you—to whom he is all the world," said the Canon's daughter, who was young and romantic, having lived upon church music and Coventry Patmore's poetry.

"There's my aunt showing them patterns of my frocks!" exclaimed Suzette, irritably, glancing in at the drawing-room, where Mrs. Mornington sat, the centre of a little group, handing scraps of stuff out of her reticule.

The scraps were being passed round and peered at and pulled about by everybody, with a meditative and admiring air. An African savage, seeing the group, would have supposed that some act of sortilege was being performed.

"It is rather an ordeal being married," said the Canon's daughter, thinking sadly of a certain undergraduate who was down-hearted about his divinity exam., and upon whose achieving deacon's orders within a reasonable time depended the young lady's matrimonial prospects.

She sighed as she thought of the difference in worldly wealth between that well-meaning youth and Allan Carew; and yet here was the future Mrs. Carew pale and worried, and obviously dissatisfied with her lot.

When those gowns had been ordered, Suzette felt as if it were another link forged in the iron chain which seemed to weigh heavier upon her every day of her life.

She had promised, and she must keep her promise. That was what she was continually saying to herself. Those words were woven into all her thoughts. Allan was so good, so true-hearted! Could she disappoint and grieve him? Could she be heartless, unkind, selfish—think of herself first and of him after—snatch at the happiness Fate offered her, and leave him out in the cold? No, better that she should bear her lot—become his wife, live out her slow, melancholy days, his faithful servant and friend, honouring him and obeying him, doing all that woman can do for man, except loving him.

Those meteoric appearances of Geoffrey's had made life much harder for Suzette. She might have fought against her love for him more successfully perhaps had he been always near; had she seen him almost daily, and become accustomed to his presence as a common incident in the daily routine; but to be told that he was in the far north of Scotland, yachting with a friend; and then to be startled by his voice at her shoulder, murmuring her name in Discombe Wood; and to turn round with nervous quickness to see him looking at her with his pale smile, like a ghost—or to be assured that he was salmon-fishing in Connemara, and to see him suddenly sauntering across the lawn in the July dusk, more ghostlike even than in the woods, as if face and form were a materialization which her own sad thoughts had conjured out of the twilight.

He would take very little trouble to explain his unlooked-for return. Scotland was too hot; the North Sea suggested a vast sheet of red-hot iron, blown over by a south wind that was like the breath of a blast-furnace. Ireland was a place of bad inns and inexorable rain; and there were no fish, or none that he could catch. He had come home because life was weariness away from home. He feared that life meant weariness everywhere.

The days were hurrying by, and now Mrs. Mornington talked everlastingly of the wedding, or so it seemed to Suzette, who in these latter days tried to avoid her aunt as much as was consistent with civility, and fled from the Grove to Discombe as to a haven of peace. Mrs. Mornington loved to expatiate upon the coming event, to bewail her niece's indifferentism, to regret that there was to be no festivity worth speaking of, and to enlarge upon the advantages of Allan's position and surroundings, and Suzette's good fortune in having come to Matcham.

"Your father might have spent a thousand pounds on a London season, and not have done half so well for you," she said conclusively.

The General nodded assent.

Certainly, between them they had done wonderfully well for Suzette.

From this worldly wisdom the harassed girl fled to the quiet of Discombe, where the peaceful silence was only broken by the deep broad stream of sound from the organ, touched with ever-growing power by Mrs. Wornock. Suzette would steal softly into the music-room unannounced, and take her accustomed seat in the recess by the organ, and sit silently listening as long as Mrs. Wornock cared to play. Only when the last chord had died away did the two women touch hands and look at each other.

It was about a week after that wearying day in Salisbury when Suzette seated herself by the player in this silent way, and sat listening to a funeral march by Beethoven, with her head leaning on her hand, and not so much as a murmur of praise for music or performer stirring the thoughtful quiet of her lips. When the last pianissimo notes, dropping to deepest bass, had melted into silence, Mrs. Wornock looked up and saw Suzette's face bathed in tears—tears that streamed over the pallid cheeks unchecked.

Geoffrey's mother started up from the organ, and clasped the weeping girl to her breast.

"Poor child! poor child! He was right, then? You are not happy."

"Happy! I am miserable! I don't know what to do. I don't know what would be worst or wickedest. To disappoint him, or to marry him, not loving him!"

"No, no, no! you must not marry, not if you cannot love him. But you are sure of that, Susie? Are you sure you don't love him? He is so good, so worthy to be loved, as his father was—years ago. Why should you not love him?"

"Ah, who can tell?" sighed Suzette. "Who knows why love begins, or how love gets the mastery? I let myself be talked into thinking I loved him. I always liked him—liked his company—was grateful for his attentions, respected him for his fine nature, and then I let him persuade me that this was love; but it wasn't—it never was love. Friendship and liking are not love; and now that the fatal day draws near I know how wide a difference there is between love and liking."

"You must not marry him, Suzette. You know I would not willingly say one word that would tell against Allan Carew's happiness. I love him almost as dearly as I love my own son; but when I see you miserable—when I see Geoffrey utterly wretched, I can no longer keep silence. This marriage must be broken off."

"Allan will hate me; he will despise me. What can he think me?—false, fickle, unworthy of a good man's love."

"You must tell him the truth. It will be cruel, but not so cruel as to let him go on believing in you, thinking himself happy, living in a fool's paradise. Will you let me speak for you, Suzette?—let me do what your mother might have done had she been here to help you in your need?"

Suzette was speechless with tears, her face hidden on Mrs. Wornock's shoulder. The door was opened at this moment, and the butler announced Mr. Carew.

Allan had approached the group by the organ before either Mrs. Wornock or Suzette could hide her agitation. Their tears, the way in which they clung to each other, told of some over-mastering grief.

"Good God! what is the matter? What has happened?" he exclaimed.

"Nothing has happened, Allan; yet there is sorrow for all of us—sorrow that has been coming upon us, though some of us did not know it. Suzette, may I tell him—now, this moment?"

"May you tell me? Tell me what?" questioned Allan. "Suzette, speak to me—you—you—no one else!"

Fear, indignation, despair were in his tone. He caught hold of Suzette's arm, and drew her towards him, looking searchingly at the pale, tear-stained face; but she shrank from his grasp, and sank on her knees at his feet.

"It is my miserable secret—that must be told at last. I have tried—I have hoped—I honour—I respect you—Allan. But our hearts are not our own; we cannot guide or govern their impulses. My heart is weighed down with shame and misery, but it is empty of love. I cannot love you as your wife should. If I keep my word, I shall be a miserable woman."

"You shall not be that," he said sternly—"not to make me the happiest man in creation. But don't you think," with chilling deliberation, "this tragedy might have been acted a little earlier? It seems to me that you have kept your secret over carefully."

"I have been weak, Allan, hopelessly, miserably weak-minded. I tried to do what was best. I did not want to disappoint you— —"

"Disappoint me? Why, you have fooled me from the first! Disappoint me? Why, I have built the whole fabric of my future life upon this rotten foundation! I was to be happy because of your love; my days and years were to flow sweetly by in a paradise of domestic peace, blest by your love. And all the time there was no such thing. You did not love me; you had never loved me; you were only trying to love me; and the hopelessness of the endeavour is brought home to you now—at this eleventh hour—three weeks before our wedding-day. Suzette, Suzette, never was woman's cruelty crueller than this of yours!"

She was in floods of tears at his feet, her head drooping till her brow almost touched the ground. He left her kneeling there, and rushed away to the garden to hide his own tears—the tears of which his manhood was ashamed, the passionate sobs, the wild hysterical weeping of the sex that seldom weeps. He found a shelter and a hiding-place in an angle of the garden, where there was a side walk shut in by close-cropped cypress walls, and here Mrs. Wornock found him presently, sitting on a marble bench, with his elbows on his knees, his face hidden in his hands.

She seated herself at his side, and laid her hand gently on his.

"Allan, dear Allan, I am so sorry for you," she said softly.

"I am very sorry for myself. I don't seem to need anybody's pity. I think I can do all the grieving."

"Ah, that is the worst of it. Nobody's sympathy can help you."

"Not yours," he answered almost savagely; "for, at heart, you must be glad. My dismissal makes room for some one else—some one whose interests are dearer to you than mine could ever be."

"There is no one nearer or dearer to me than you, Allan—no one—not even my own son. You have been to me as a son—the son of the man I fondly loved, whose face I was to look upon only once—once after those long years in which we were parted. I have loved you as a part of my youth, the living memory of my lost love. Ah, my dear, I had to learn the lesson of self-surrender when I was younger than you. I loved him with all my heart and mind, and I gave him up."

"You did wrong to give him up. He himself said so. But there is no parallel between the two cases. This girl has let me believe in her. I have lived for a year in this sweet delusion—a bliss no more real than the happiness of a dream. She would have loved me; she would have married me; all would have been well for us but for your son. When he came, my chance was blighted. He has charms of mind and manner which I have not—like me, they say, but ten times handsomer. He can speak to her with a language that I have not. Oh, those singing notes on the violin; that long-drawn lingering sweep of the bow, like the cry of a spirit in paradise—an angelic voice telling of love ethereal—love released from clay; those tears which seemed to tremble on the strings; that loud, sudden sob of passionate pain, which came like a short, sharp amen to the prayer of love! I could understand that language better than he thought. He stole her love from me—set himself deliberately to rob me of my life's happiness."

"It is cruel to say that, Allan. He is incapable of treachery, of deliberate wrong-doing. He is a creature of impulse."

"Meaning a creature with whom self is the only god. And in one of his impulses he told Suzette of his love, even in plainer words than his Stradivarius could tell the story; and from that hour her heart was false to me. I saw the change in her when I came back—after my father's death."

"You are unjust to him, Allan, in your grief and anger. Whatever his feelings may have been, he has fought against them. He has made himself almost an exile from this house."

"He has been biding his time, no doubt; and now that I have had the *coup de grace* he will come back."

CHAPTER XII
"THAT WAY MADNESS LIES"

It would have taken a very respectable earthquake to have made as much sensation in a rural neighbourhood as was made in the village and neighbourhood of Matcham by the cancelment of Allan Carew's engagement to General Vincent's daughter. The fact that no visitors had been bidden to the wedding seemed to make no difference in the rapid dissemination of the news. People from twenty miles round had been interested; people from twenty miles round had come up to be taxed, and had sent pepper-pots and hair-brushes, paper-knives and scent-bottles, fans and candlesticks—all of which were now returned to the givers in the very tissue paper and cardboard boxes in which they had been sent from shops or stores, accompanied by a formal little note of apology. The marriage had been deferred indefinitely; and, at his daughter's request, General Vincent begged to return the gifts, with best thanks for the kindly feeling which had prompted, etc.

"It will do for some one else!"

That was the almost inevitable exclamation when the tissue paper was unfolded and the gift appeared, untarnished and undamaged by the double transit. Then followed speculations as to the meaning of those words, "deferred indefinitely."

"Indefinitely means never," pronounced Mrs. Roebuck; "there's no doubt upon that point. He has jilted her. I thought he would begin to look about him after his father's death. I dare say he will have a house in town next season—a *pied à terre* near Park Lane and go into society, instead of vegetating among those Bœotians. He must feel himself thrown away in such a hole."

"I thought he was devoted to Miss Vincent."

"Nonsense! How could any man be devoted to an insignificant Frenchified chit without style or *savoir farie*?"

"She has a pretty, piquant little face," murmured Mr. Roebuck meekly, not liking to be enthusiastic about beauty which was the very opposite of his wife's Roman-nosed and flaxen-haired style.

Upon Mrs. Mornington the blow fell far more heavily than on Suzette's father, who was very glad to keep his daughter at home, albeit regretful that she should have treated a faithful lover so scurvily.

"If the poor child did not know her own mind at the beginning, it's a blessed thing she found out her mistake before it was too late," pleaded the General to his irate sister.

"It *is* too late—too late for respectability—too late for common humanity. To lead a young man on for over a year, almost to the foot of the altar, and then to throw him off. It is simply shameful! To make a fool of him and herself before the whole neighbourhood—to belittle herself as much as she has belittled him. No doubt all the women will say that *he* has jilted *her*."

"Let them. That cannot hurt her."

"But it can hurt me, her aunt. I feel inclined to slap my most intimate friends when they ask me leading questions, evidently longing to hear that Allan has acted badly. And when I assure them that my niece is alone to blame, I can see in their faces that they don't, or won't, believe me. And why should they believe me? Could any girl, not an idiot, throw over such a match as Allan has become since his father's death?"

"I hope you don't mean to say that my girl is an idiot?"

"I say that she has acted like an idiot in this affair."

"And I say that she has acted like an honest woman."

"I shall never be able to look Lady Emily Carew in the face again."

"Don't be alarmed about Lady Emily. She will be no more sorry to keep her son to herself than I am to keep my daughter."

"She won't have him long. He'll be going off and marrying some horrid end-of-the-century girl in a fit of pique."

"I don't believe he is such a fool."

Matcham might talk its loudest, and dispute almost to blows, as to which was the jilter and which the jilted. The principal performers in the tragedy were well out of ear-shot—Allan at Fendyke with Lady Emily, Suzette at Bournemouth with an old convent friend and her invalid mother, people who had no connection with Matcham, and in whose society the girl could not be reminded of her own wrong-doing. The invitation to the villa at Branksome had been repeated very often; and on a renewal of it arriving just after that painful scene at Discombe, Suzette had written promptly to accept.

"If you don't mind my coming to you out of spirits and altogether troubled in mind, *chérie*," she wrote; and the girl, who was a very quiet piece of amiability, and who had worshipped her livelier school-fellow, replied delightedly, "Your low spirits must be brighter than other people's gaiety. Come, and let the sea and the downs console you. Bournemouth is lovely in September. Mother has given me the charmingest pony, and I have been carefully taught by our old coachman, who is a whip in a thousand, so you need not be afraid to trust yourself beside me."

"Except for father's sake, it might be a good thing if she were to throw me out of her cart and kill me on the spot," mused Suzette, as she sat listlessly watching her maid packing her trunk.

Among the frocks, there was one of the Salisbury tailor's confections, a frock which was to have been worn by Mrs. Allan Carew, and Suzette felt that she would sink with shame when she put it on.

"I ought to be prosecuted for obtaining goods under false pretences," she thought.

Geoffrey Wornock found a telegram waiting for him at the little post-office at Hartzburg, and the mere outward casing of that message set his heart beating furiously. There must be news of his love in it, news good or bad.

"I will not live through her wedding-day, if she marries him," he told himself.

The telegram was from his mother.

"The marriage is broken off with much sorrow on both sides."

"That's nonsense. On her part there can be no sorrow—only relief of mind, only joy, the prospect of a blissful union, a life without a cloud. Thank God, thank God, thank God! I never felt there was a God till now. Now I believe in Him—now I will lift up my heart to Him, in nightly and daily prayer, as Adam did by the side of Eve. Oh, thank God, the barrier is removed, and she can be mine! My own dear love—heart of my heart—life of my life!"

He carried a fiddle among his scanty luggage, not the treasured inimitable Stradivarius, but a much-cherished little Amati; and by-and-by, having eaten some hurried scraps by way of dinner, he took the violin out of its case and went out to a little garden at the back of the inn, and in a vine-clad berceau gave himself up to impassioned utterance of the love that overflowed his heart. Music, and music only, could speak for him—music was the interpreter of all his highest thoughts. The stolid beer-drinkers came out of their smoke-darkened parlour to hear him, and sat silent and unseen behind an intervening screen of greenery, and listened and approved.

"Ach, what for a fiddler! How he can play! Whole heaven-like. Not true, my friend?"

He played and played, walking about under the vine-curtain—played till the pale grey evening shadows darkened to purple night, and the stars looked through the leafy roof of that rustic tunnel. He was playing to her; to her, his far-away love; to Suzette in England. He was pouring out his soul's desire to her, a hymn of sweet content; and he almost fancied that she could hear him. There must be some mystical medium by which such sounds can travel from being to being, where love attunes two souls in unison—some process now hidden from the dull mind of average man, as the electric telegraph was half a century ago.

This is how a lover dreams in the summer gloaming, in a garden on the slope of a pine-clad hill, with loftier heights beyond, shadowy and dark against the deep blue of that infinite sky where the stars are shining aloof and incomprehensible, in remoteness that fills mortality with despair.

She was free! That was Geoffrey's one thought in every hour and almost every minute of his breathless journey from Hartzburg to Discombe. She was free; and for her to be free meant that she was to be his. He imagined no opposition upon her side when once her engagement to Allan had been broken. She had been bound by that tie, and that only. His impetuous, passionate nature, self-loving and concentrative as the temper of a child, could conceive no restraining influence, nothing that could prevent her heart answering his, her hand yielding to his, and a marriage as speedy as law and Church would allow.

They could be married ever so quietly—in London—where no curious eyes could watch, no gossiping tongues criticise—married—made for ever one; and then away to mountain and lake, to Pallanza, Lugano, Bellaggio, to flowery shores betwixt hill and water, to a life lovelier than his fairest dreams.

No man journeying with a passionate heart ever found rail or boat quick enough, and Geoffrey, always impatient, chafed at every stage of the journey, and complained as bitterly as if he had been travelling at the expensive crawl in which a Horace Walpole or a Beckford was content to accomplish that restricted round which our ancestors called the "grand tour." Nothing slower than a balloon driving before a gale would have satisfied Geoffrey's eager soul. And he would rather have accepted balloon transit, with all its hazards, and run the risk of being landed in a Carinthian valley or a Norwegian fjord, than endure the harassing delay at dusty railway stations, or the slowness of the channel boat.

He telegraphed to his mother from Brussels, and again from Dover; so there was a cart waiting for him at the station with one of the fastest horses in the stable, but, unfortunately, one of the stupidest grooms, who could furnish him with no information upon any subject.

Was all well at home? His mistress well?

The groom believed so.

"Was Miss Vincent well?"

The groom had heard nothing to the contrary; but he had not seen Miss Vincent lately.

No particular inference was to be drawn from this statement of the groom's, since Suzette's visits were not made to the stableyard.

There was no one at Discombe to do stable-parade and to insist upon horses being stripped and trotted up and down for the edification of a visitor whose utmost knowledge of a horse might be that it is a beast with four legs—mane and tail understood, though not always existent.

Geoffrey rattled his old hunter along at a pace that made the cart sway like an outrigger in the wake of a steamer, and he alighted at the Manor House at least a quarter of an hour before a reasonable being would have got himself there.

It was late in the evening, and his mother was sitting alone in the dimly lighted music-room. The piano was shut—a bad sign; for when Suzette was there the piano was hardly ever idle.

"Well, mother dear, so glad to be home again," said Geoffrey, with an affectionate hug, but with eyes that were looking over his mother's head into space for another presence, even while he gave her that filial embrace.

"And I am so glad to have you, Geoffrey; and I hope now this restless spirit will be content to stay."

"*C'est selon.* Where's Suzette?"

"At Bournemouth, with an old school-fellow."

"Why didn't you wire her address, and then I could have gone straight to her?"

"My dear Geoffrey, what are you thinking of?"

"Of Suzette—of my dear love—of my wife that is to be!"

"My dear boy, you cannot go to her. You must not ask her to marry you while this cancelled engagement is a new thing. I should think her a horrid girl if she would listen to you—for ever so long."

"Do you mean for a week—or a fortnight?"

"For a long, long time, Geoffrey—long enough for Allan's wounded heart to recover."

"Upon my soul, mother, that is too good a joke! Is my mother, the most romantic and unconventional of women, preaching the eighteenpenny gospel of middle-class etiquette?"

"It is no question of conventionality. My affection for Allan is only second to my love for you, and I cannot bear to think of his being wounded and humiliated, as he must be if Suzette were to accept you directly after having jilted him."

"And you would have Suzette sit beside the tomb of Allan's hopes for a year or so while I eat my heart out—banquet on joys deferred—sicken and die, perhaps, with that slow torture of waiting. Mother, you don't know what love is—love in the heart of a man. If she had married Allan, I should have shot myself on her wedding-day. That was written in my book of fate. If she won't marry me; if she play fast and loose, blow hot, blow cold; if she won't look in my eyes and say honestly, 'I love you,' and 'I am yours,' I can't answer for myself—I fear there will be a tragedy. You know there is something here"—touching his forehead—"which loses itself in a whirl of fiery confusion when this"—touching his heart—"is too sorely tried."

"Geoffrey, my dearest! oh, Geoffrey, you agonize me when you talk like that! I think—yes, I believe that Suzette loves you; but she is sensitive, tender-hearted—all that is womanly and good. You must give her time to recover from the shock of parting with Allan, whom she sincerely esteems, and whose sorrow is her sorrow."

"I will see her to-morrow. I cannot live without seeing her. Why, every mile of pine-forest through which I came seemed three, every mile of dusty Belgian flatness seemed seven, to my hot impatience. I must see her, hear her, hold her hand in mine; and she shall do what she likes with the poor rag of life which will be left when I have lived an hour with her."